Ahmam's Islands

Translated from Taiwanese

I0617594

CHUNG WENYIN

TRANSLATED BY
CJ Anderson Wu

EDITED BY
Steven M Anderson

PUBLISHING

ISBN 9780982140796
P.R.A. Publishing
P.O. Box 211701
Martinez, Georgia 30917
U.S.A.
www.prapublishing.com

First printing
Copyright © Chung Wenyin 2006
Serenity International,
Taipei, Taiwan

Translation from Taiwanese to English by C.J. Anderson Wu. Edited by Steven M. Anderson. Woman's Island published in English in 2010. Translation renamed Ahmam's Island in 2012.

*This book is dedicated to all mothers
and sisters who are struggling.*

and

*To my family, for their longtime
support of my writing career.*

Acknowledgments

The publication of the English edition of *Woman Islands* should be credited to many. The first person I should thank is Mr. Chung Tsuang-Shan a rice farmer from my hometown, Yunlin. When he heard how much it costs for my book to be translated into English, he calculated how much rice he could harvest and sell to raise this money. The rice he donated was the most delicious food I ever had, and I believe all the people who purchased his rice in response to this project feel the same way. This way of involving so many in raising funds for literature is unprecedented. Ms. Kao Dan-Hua, the section chief of the Yunlin County Government, promoted the sale of the donated rice at many other events to raise awareness and support for the publication of this book. This book wouldn't have been accomplished without her creative ideas and hard work.

I want to thank two of my friends, Elly Chou and May Chen, as well as the Hakka Village. The Five House Community Association sponsored me when they saw the story about the rice donation in the newspaper, so in addition to translating and editing fee, we also have the money for layout design and printing. The bureau head of the Department of Urban and Rural Planning of the Yunlin County Government, Mr. Chen Chang-Hsien, also helped me with as many resources as he could find in his department, even though literature and planning are two independent affairs. I also want to thank C.J. and Steve. Ever since they decided to translate my works, we have become very good friends. Finally, I hope this book will echo in your minds, my dear readers.

Note from the Translator

The status of women in Taiwan is very tricky. They are encouraged to be independent and own businesses, but they are also expected to fulfill all kinds of traditional family obligations, including continuing the family line by giving birth to boys. Such a peculiar condition for Taiwanese women probably developed through the course of the social and political chaos of Taiwan's past. Women were forced to make crucial decisions and be the breadwinners for their families when their husbands and fathers were either dead or imprisoned. Women had to take on the male roles. This is the case with the family of the protagonist, Ahmam, in the novel *Woman's Island*. Ahmam's mother worked hard to survive when she was a young wife; her irresponsible husband's drinking problem meant that he couldn't support the family at all. Ahmam's memories about her father were sweet rather than disappointed, especially when compared to her mother's furious thoughts. Despite feeling betrayed and deceived all her life, Ahmam's mother tried to make everything right for her family. But this hovering concern resulted in a deep dissatisfaction with Ahmam's situation, especially her unmarried status. This sort of mother/daughter tension remains a very common phenomenon in Taiwan even today—women who have themselves suffered so much in marriage still think that every woman should get married. Unemployed, single, and penniless, Ahmam perfectly matched the profile of a loser, so a trip home for a family reunion during the Chinese New Year holidays was a torment for her. During the short trip home, Ahmam reviewed her life and her relationship to her family, seeing her life history compressed into a few days.

As a reader, *Woman's Islands* reminds me of the later part of Virginia Woolf's **To the Lighthouse**, as flashes of memories across a considerable time span are quickly retrieved and stowed away by the author. In this small world, women share the same fate. Married or not married, having offspring or not, accomplishing a lot in the city or not, every woman is an island, alone in the ocean.

Woman's Island was first published in 1998. It is Chung Wenyin's first novel, and the experience writing it was when she finally realized that, instead of a marriage or a job with stable income, writing was the only way for her to live. This book was semi-autobiographical, and the dozens of novels Chung has completed since have also been. In an interview, she said she liked to mix her own experience into her novels. The character of Ahmam's mother was actually very close to Chung's own mother;

they still exchange very opposite opinions about life, marriage, and family to this day. Chung's latest project is an ambitious trilogy that zooms out from her family history to the traumatic events in Taiwan over the past century. This trilogy consists of the titles *Decayed Lust*, *A Short Song*, and *A Sorrowful Song*. *Decayed Lust* was published in 2006, *A Short Song* was published in 2010, and *A Sorrowful Song* will be published in 2011. These stories are told in three big volumes and contain more than one million Chinese characters in all

Translating Chung Wenyin is very challenging because she uses words in a unique style that mixes oral Taiwanese language and Mandarin as well as using many inventive turns of phrase. Chung likes to use puns, and the translator has to find the best way to make them contain the same flavor in English. Of course, there are still many aspects of Chung's profound style that remain untranslatable, and the translator has attempted to modify them without changing too much of the author's intention.

Readers might find the writing style of Chung quite unusual, which is even more obvious in her later works than in this first volume. For the English translation, Chung insisted on maintaining the awkwardness of her writing instead of completely smoothing it out for English readers. The author's wish is consistent with a strain in postcolonial translation theory that suggests an eroticizing style is the best way to show the author's and translator's resistance against dominant languages. Taiwanese literature has seldom been translated into English literature from a small culture hardly gets noticed in the larger book market. Over the past decades, few Taiwanese literary novels have been translated into other languages, and most of them were works from a long time ago. Additionally, most of the English translation of Taiwanese literature has been done by English-speaking translators who certainly would not resist their own language as some translation theorists urge nonnative English translators to do. As a woman growing up in an environment very similar to that of the author, the translator took up the task with audacity. If readers find any fault in the English, the responsibility is the translator's. The author, translator, and editor hope the English edition of *Woman Islands* represents an intriguing introduction to modern Taiwanese literature for the English-speaking audience.

C.J. Anderson-Wu is the editor of *Taiwan Architect Magazine Woman Islands*/Ahmam's Islands, is her third translation of a Taiwanese novel. She recently helped publish **Decayed Lust** by Chung Wenyin.

Ahmam

Ahmam couldn't remember when she began to crave a life without any regulations or expectations. She wished, for instance, on an unbearably hot afternoon that she was able to make time freeze. Over the past months, Ahmam had gone to bed late and gotten up late. It had been that way since last November. On many nights she'd sit up for no reason until around three or four o'clock in the morning and unconsciously touch the scar on her back. Then, amid the roar of the elevator that could be heard through the shoddy walls of her apartment, Ahmam crashed again.

Only one man could wake her up before noon-time—the old man selling salty daikon cakes. The street peddler hawked at the entrance of Ahmam's alley, she drooled as she heard his calls

1

break through her dreams. If anyone had glanced at her at that moment, they might have assumed Ahmam was flooded by yearning for her lover. Ahmam could always detect the unpredictable arrival of the old man. She'd rummage in the iron cookie box for coins and sluggishly put on a coat inside out before going downstairs to find the old man. The hot, shredded daikon stuffed in the cakes never failed to completely wake her up when her tongue finally touched it. Ahmam was glad that her mother never saw her in this manner. She had no problem imagining what her mother would say: "What a loser—just like your loser father."

The alluring smell of cakes stirred her as she approached the peddler; she became conscious gradually. Compared to other buyers who were dressed up formally for work, Ahmam looked like a kid ditching class on a whim. She observed the old man kneading the dough into a round, thin sheet and stuff flavored daikon shreds into it. The dough became a small mound, not unlike the breast of a woman. Then the old man's wrinkled and freckled palms pressed it flat before dropping it into the oily frying pan.

The old man pointed at Ahmam with his flour-whitened finger, and Ahmam answered "two" with her voice still hoarse from sleep. Two cakes were actually too much for her, but she found it embarrassing to buy just one. Other people bought a lot more, and she didn't want to admit that she was just feeding herself. Thus she always swallowed the first cake, then took several bites of the second, and before she got too full to eat more, she'd struggle to take one or two more bites. She put down the unfinished cake beside her bed and crawled back in her blanket to continue her sleep. Ahmam liked to pull the blanket all the way up to her face. Only her exposed forehead reflected the red light of the electric heater's quartz tubes.

Today the old man didn't come, Ahmam got up unusually early. She tore off the old page on the daily wall calendar, twisting quite hard. As yesterday flipped away, paper crumbs fluttered like white hair in the breeze. In addition to the red, blue, and green numbers of the month, date and day, the Chinese characters announced that the north direction was inauspicious today, and people born in the years of snake should be especially careful.

The ground floor of the building was a car repair business, but the daily mechanic noises weren't there today. It reminded Ahmam that it was the day before New Year's Eve and everyone was back home for the reunion feast. The shouts from the Tae Kwon Do school downstairs were also gone. From the absolute silence of the entire building, Ahmam knew that all her roommates were back home; one of them had even taken the cat home.

Usually the white cat, Mimi, would scurry aimlessly among the cardboard boxes in the sitting room or slink past the drape hung over Ahmam's door. She'd approach Ahmam's bed and scratch the wooden floor with her sharp claws, totally ignoring the existence of her mistress. Ahmam's roommate Tziyang would do aerobic exercise at home on rainy days, the worn wooden floorboards flipping up and down as she jumped. After several quiet moments, another roommate, Yingdan, a stout girl, would come out from another door. Yingdan liked to make crunchy sandwiches in the months before October because that was the time cucumbers and carrots tasted best. She seldom forgot to appreciate the wonderful vegetables, saying, "I wish these delicious things could be harvested year round."

When the cucumbers and carrots were not in season, Yingdan ate instant oat soup. She'd add an egg yolk to the soup and put the egg white over her face, her daily beauty routine. One evening not so long ago, Yingdan dined with her boyfriend and ordered a sandwich that was obviously expensive. When the dinner was over and they said good-bye to each other, the boyfriend called the same evening and said since they had very different values, they should have separate lives. "Different values! He insisted on paying the bill and then regretted he had paid it," Yingdan said angrily. That night, Ahmam, whose room was next to the bathroom, couldn't sleep because Yingdan was determined to throw up the sandwich that had resulted in the end of her relationship.

The room by the corridor was empty. One month ago its former occupant, Xufang, got married and moved out. Xufang kept her claim on the room and bade them to keep it as she wasn't sure that her marriage would last very long. Ahmam and the other roommates teased Xufang saying that the money in the red envelopes for her wedding should be cut in half in order to match her short-lived marriage. On her wedding day, Xufang could not stop sobbing; she was like a rainy December day. Her mother in-law must have thought that Xufang was attached to her birth family very tightly, and her son must feel lucky that his bride was a woman from the old school.

Xufang's marriage had been short lived. On the night of her birthday in April, a phone call from overseas changed everything. Her husband, stationed in Germany, unexpectedly told her he was marrying the next day instead of wishing her happy birthday. Xufang hung up the phone and kicked her door with all the strength she had. All the roommates agreed that Xufang was entitled to break things so her agony would be at least partially alleviated. Ever since that night, her door would never quite shut right.

Now Ahmam sat at the edge of her bed. She wore a man's white cotton shirt that was baggy on her. She listened to the chilly air; as the wind gusts blew over the door, they made a sound not unlike sighs. Ahmam could feel the sounds and the colors around her in the air, and then she lifted her blue blanket covering the flower-patterned sheet. The sheet was five years old, Ahmam used it as a cover before she was given the blue one this winter. The heaviness of the old one and the lightness of the blue one made a contrast. The blue blanket was a present from her last lover; the old, rosy one was then downgraded to the position of a sheet. She got it from her ex-boyfriend Linzhan when he left for his mandatory service in the military. The cotton had been pressed into thick chunks and became so dense it was no longer effective at keeping in warmth. But the blue one was made of fresh cotton mixed with silk; it wrapped the body tenderly and felt like nothing but fondness.

Between the new and old blankets, there had been two lovers. Ahmam sneezed like she was allergic to the turning of the New Year. Instead of blowing her nose, she grasped a facial oil absorbent paper from a box decorated with the Chinese character double blessing to wipe her face. The paper turned translucent immediately from the oil her face secreted at night. Ahmam looked at herself in the mirror and was shocked at how she looked in the morning. Her eyes were like those of dead fish, and the muscles around her nose made deep lines. She moved closer to the mirror to scrutinize her still-sleepy face more carefully and made an expression that again revealed her shock at her own image. Ahmam liked her complexion at night better. Somehow she felt that her delicate eyes, nose, and lips looked better proportioned before she went to bed. But there was usually no one to see her then. Ahmam also resented her name; she thought it was too vulgar for a beautiful woman. A painting of the twelve animals of the Chinese zodiac hung over an east-facing window to block sunlight. Ahmam had arranged a traditional paper cutting of a pair of birds clutching lilies over the window facing west. Since the windows were not lit by natural light, Ahmam illuminated them with a lamp.

Above the lamp was a paper lantern from the Lantern Festival the previous year. She and Tziyang had mixed themselves with the crowd of youth in the park that night. In her hometown, there were fireflies everywhere. Compared to the artificial illumination in an urban park, the lighted tails of the fireflies were seductive. Although she was single now, Ahmam knew a good night's sleep usually came from love—not only love in the heart, but also lovemaking. When she had a lover to share the bed with, her body would be emancipated, even partially dismantled, by the violent movements and screams, and then she'd lay paralyzed in bed, like a collapsed house.

That's why the daytime was like a curse to Ahmam. Her dry eyes told her it was still early and she looked up at the clock hanging on the wall. It pointed to three o'clock, she remembered then that the previous night in her tossing and turning, she had decided the ticking was annoying, so she had stood on a chair and taken out the battery. No wonder it swallowed the *Ohayo*—"Good Morning" in Japanese—this morning. The pig-shaped clock looked cuter to Ahmam now that it was no longer able to make any noise.

Ahmam slightly tore a corner of the animal painting to peep out of the window; flimsy light poked out from the sky. She heard some muffled voices from the blockish apartments attached to her building, suggesting restrained pleasure. Low, hoarse music from someone's radio seemed to play out of tune. Suddenly, an explosion of fire-crackers surprised Ahmam and scared away a few birds perched on a nearby power pole.

Ahmam got up and took her toothbrush and toothpaste from an apple green basin. The toothpaste was strawberry flavored, a cartoon-themed toothpaste for kids. She also picked up the pink trash bag lying on the floor, considered for a moment and, still holding her toothbrush, walked to a corner and jumped up several times to pull off the dried-rose bouquet hung upside down from the ceiling. The roses had turned maroon, she squeezed them into the trash bag and trudged in her big slippers to the illegally built balcony on the seventh floor of the ten-year-old apartment, where she could see the intersection below. There was a trash chute built into the wall of the balcony, so Ahmam dropped the trash bag in and heard: plop! The trash bag had hit the bottom. It would be taken away by a trash truck after midnight. Once in a while, Ahmam would step out on the balcony to check out the drivers opening the door of the trash dumpster and moving the bags to the black slit at the back of the truck one by one. Yingdan and the other room-mates were sure Ahmam was crazy. Those trash haulers were old and poorly paid for a stinky job; what was it about them that made them worth Ahmam's enthusiastic observation in the middle of the night? Aware they were being watched, the garbage men chatted amongst themselves. "Girls in Taipei never go to sleep; they just fool around all night long." Some of them were convinced that Ahmam was enduring a heartbreaking relationship and thus couldn't fall asleep. Ahmam's behavior at least gave them something to talk about.

If you drove into that intersection around nightfall and happened to lift your head to look at the balcony while stuck in traffic, you might see Ahmam sitting in the bone-piercing cold before the sky was entirely submerged in darkness. Blown by the wind, her thick hair would be flying like the wings of angels. Her face would shine from the red lights of the taller buildings nearby. Ahmam didn't know why she loved being there at that time so much; the only reason she could think of was the comfort an unemployed person gets from seeing others hurry home after a long day.

As Ahmam brushed her teeth, the foam of the toothpaste dropped onto the rusted, fragile rail. December was a rainy month; the humid cold days around New Year's hurried one to age faster. While all her roommates were gone at work in the morning, Ahmam often counted the raindrops she heard on the roof. She was like a king living in his own castle alone; taking orders from himself. One morning while she was listening to the raindrops, she heard a stray dog cry miserably. Ahmam shed a tear for the homeless helpless dog.

It's hard to deal with the rainy season, but it's no easier in the summer. Their house could barely protect them from the burning sun; the heat seemed able to drill through the walls and torture them directly. Occasionally a torrential rain on a summer night would make Ahmam's room on the end of the corridor drip here and there while she lay sleeping. She had to get up and save her clothes from a soaked closet. On one bright summer day following a heavy rain, Ahmam tidied up the scattered clothes into the finally dry closet and flipped over her tatami to expose it to some ultraviolet rays. When it was turned over, Ahmam was shocked by the numerous bugs that had been living with her for who knows how long. Looking at the ugly, squirming aliens, the hair all over Ahmam's body stood up. She never forgot the creepy experience. The side of her tatami had been soaked too long; nonetheless, she couldn't afford a new one.

Her days dragged on into the winter. The beginning of the new year of the solar calendar, or the end of the old year of the lunar calendar, was the coldest time. After the last period in what is known in the lunar calendar as the Big Chill, there was usually a cold front in which every gust of wind brought in nippy air, and that air made Ahmam's tatami icy like a coffin.

The landlady had their apartment repaired only once, when the leaking water infiltrated through the ceiling downstairs and dropped on her baby's face. She blamed the tenants for not appreciating their shared property. Yingdan was enraged at the landlady's remarks, and they quarreled. Ahmam buried her head in a book during the fight, which infuriated Yingdan even more. She hated Ahmam for not speaking out for justice. Yingdan shut her door in Ahmam's face. Ahmam wished she could help in the confrontation, but her cowardice always pulled her away from really coming forward in any argument. Reading was her way of dodging conflicts.

It was difficult to find where the leaking started, the water had eroded almost everything; the apartment never got any improvements. The landlady found a way to ignore it and Ahmam, who could not really afford any other place in Taipei, had no choice but to hope the damage in the next rainy season would be less severe.

On her balcony, Ahmam rubbed her face with cleaning foam as she watched the housewife on the balcony in the opposite apartment shake a washcloth before hanging it up. Ahmam could smell the fragrance of the detergent. On another balcony, a grandma was flinging her arms around quickly in a kind of therapeutic exercise, but the shaking made her look like she was having convulsions. Her husband was trimming plants with measured movements; every now and then he stopped and his shears froze in the air. The aging couples mouths opened and their eyes went blank. To them, time lapsed and then reconnected, like a melody sung in intervals. Sometimes a baby's crying broke the spell. Or dogs invariably echoed the crying baby with their endless barking.

The people Ahmam observed turned to look at her, too, but they didn't seem to know or recognize her. As Ahmam stretched her head out of the rails to look at the Kapok tree that was almost five stories high, a drop of the foam from the facial cleaner on her cheek dripped onto one big leaf when she leaned forward. "What a coincidence," she thought to herself. Then the leaf fell away from its stem. Ahmam wondered if the leaf had decided to leave the tree as soon as it got the drop it had been waiting for. Ahmam was lost in her reverie, and the circular motions of washing her face slowed down.

The in-harmonious buildings surrounding her were ill fitted in this environment; so were the people occupying them. Ten or twenty years ago, these buildings were modern compared to the older ones without elevators. But now they were out of fashion, they were neither as fancy as the newer and taller buildings nor as nostalgic as those built earlier. Moreover, their views were becoming blocked by newer construction. Ahmam thought, "certain kinds of buildings will house particular kinds of occupants. That's why our kind of women live in this building." Ahmam hated having the people around her think that she was desperate for a mate and evaluate her for any possible matchmaking possibilities, like they were calculating the value of a product in the market. She'd rather grow old alone than fulfill their vain hope.

When Ahmam moved in, she did not know the tree crowned with green leaves was a Kapok until spring, coaxed by the warmer days, the leaves handsomely left the branches to yield space for flaming flowers. Ahmam regretted not appreciating this wonderful living treasure earlier. From the freezing winter to the torrid summer, a guy had taken care of her, like he was nourishing a plant for the next blooming season. She missed the significance of many things during that time, including him, just like she had ignored the beautiful Kapok tree all the time. In regret, Ahmam wondered how many good things she let slip through her fingers. She told herself that some things are destined to be missed no matter how hard she worked to maintain them.

The first flight in the morning took off from Songshan Airport; drawing a line above the abandoned munitions factory and its chimney. The pampas grass wildly sprawling across its roof swayed in the wind, accentuating how deserted it was. Ahmam began to feel the interesting part of being up early she rinsed her face quickly. The cold water chilled her.

If the emergence and submergence of an idea are equal to life and death, Ahmam has lived and died uncountable times.

Ahmam had very complex and inexplicable feelings about airplanes. When she was a little girl, she once hid under a gray stone column while an airplane flew across the sky. Her mother, who was cooking, rushed into the yard with a spatula in her hand and kneeled down to kowtow to the plane. She murmured prayers to the airplane solemnly. Over the horizon nightfall was breaking; rosy clouds gathered at one side of the sky, and the last few sunbeams penetrated through them. Little Ahmam wondered, "Why didn't the airplane fall?" Her bowing mother did not go back to finish her stir-frying until the airplane's tail was completely out of sight. That night their dinner tasted sandy, but no one dared to complain.

When Ahmam grew older, she was told that her mother had grown up during the war; she had spent her youth hiding from air raids all the time. Once, when she found it was too late to find any shelter as a bomber hovered above her head, she stood in the yard, dumbfounded, as the bomber took off without dropping a bomb. Ahmam's mother never forgot the face of the American pilot who turned his head to gaze at her. When all the people got back from their shelters, she stood there motionless.

Years later, Ahmam's mother stopped worship-ping airplanes; instead, Ahmam seemed to take to it. Whenever her parents were fighting, she'd hope an airplane would roar over their heads to save her from the situation.

Ahmam's childhood imagination was long gone; now airplanes only drew associations of lug-gage and foreign lands. Ahmam thought maybe she should buy fewer outfits and save some money to arrange an overseas trip for her mother, who never took an airplane nor traveled abroad. Ahmam sighed and wondered why a wish so hum-ble and so straightforward would be so impossible for both the mother and the daughter?

Across the way, in a few apartments several people who looked like the sort who had to work right through New Year's Eve began dismantling the window screens from their panes for washing, as they did their rooms became partly visible. Their movements were like a live show on a large screen, and Ahmam was the only spectator of the free performance. The sound of splashing water reminded Ahmam she still had laundry to do, she lifted the bright green basket and joined everyone else in cleaning for the New Year.

Ahmam remembered to check every pocket of her clothes before she washed them this was unusual for her. Some coins dropped on the floor, Ahmam picked them up; they were tokens from an amusement park. In another pocket she found pink tissue paper, crumpled and smelling of mustard. It was from a farewell meal with her friend Ahji; they had dined in a Japanese restaurant and talked all day.

Ahmam also found cinema tickets and some shopping receipts. Sorrowful thoughts of how time flies flooded her mind. Ahmam washed the clothes, washing away the past. Without the help of a washing machine, Ahmam's work seemed particularly difficult. She rinsed the clothes and hung them over a bamboo stick; all the clothes were like spread blackbird wings, sweating and swaying listlessly in the cold air. For quite some time Ahmam had only worn black outfits.

The sky was made gray by a cold front—at eight o'clock in the morning the day was still bleak. Ahmam's fingers were pale from washing; she sucked them unconsciously and furrowed her eyebrows with somber thoughts. She heard a young child howl because his mother slapped him on his ear. Staining clothes with a few drops of milk was such a tiny thing; why punish a kid so severely? Ahmam shook her head in confusion. The kid must have had a similar fate to hers. Such kids always fail to catch up to the tempo of adults during important events. In the supposedly cheerful atmosphere of the New Year's festivities, people like Ahmam and that poor slapped kid who had spilled the milk were clueless about why they were supposed to act the way adults expected them to. Ahmam recalled how on one New Year's Eve, she was sent by her mother to find her father. She walked around their village and found her father smoking under a big tree. He had lost money gambling and did not have the courage to come home. The image was still vivid in her mind. Ahmam looked at her inky clothes and realized she resembled her father very much. Now, she didn't have the courage to go home; the profiles of the father and daughter overlapped.

Jiachang and Juchi

Jiachang, a good friend of Ahmam's ex-boyfriend, Linzhan, was coming over sometime that day. Ahmam had sold him her stereo and refrigerator. Jiachang was giving her half the money today as a down payment, which would save Ahmam from the embarrassment of giving her mother; nieces and nephews empty red envelopes. Not only would the kids be disappointed if they didn't receive any money, Ahmam couldn't afford to lose face with her brothers and their wives. Above all, Ahmam was afraid of her mother's harsh ranting to the tune of: "If she was able to give us any money, she'd have given it to us a long time ago. Don't expect she has made any progress." Her disappointment in her children not rewarding her hard work was equal to her acrimony toward her late husband.

For quite a long time, Ahmam's only visitor was a policeman. He brought Ahmam news that she had failed to file a report on her residential registration when she moved from home. He fined her several hundred dollars. Ahmam was afflicted by the thought that the amount of money could have bought several meals. Expecting Jiachang to have arrived already, Ahmam gazed at the clock anxiously it was still not ticking. The doorbell finally rang. When Jiachang entered, he rubbed his feet on the rug. "Raining?" Ahmam asked as she took the dark red umbrella and scarf he was wearing.

"Drizzle." he replied.

His protruding nose was like a cliff; his breath cooling down in the cold air caused the fog around it. Jiachang's heart throbbed a bit when Ahmam's warm, soft hand touched his frigid palm; for a moment he felt sentimental. Seeing Ahmam gesturing for the money, Jiachang's feelings turned to disappointment. He reached his hand into his pocket slowly and said, "This money is still warm. I hate to see it go." Ahmam extended her hand for the money, so he stopped moving, wishing she would get closer. Ahmam acted like she didn't care and turned away. Jiachang couldn't help but approach her. He spoke suggestively, saying, "If it weren't you...I wouldn't need these things at all."

"Why? Ahmam exclaimed. You loved classical music in college. I remember I produced posters for your speech about Pictures at an Exhibition by Mussorgsky. When you were talking about the dwarf's awkward leaping, you looked completely enraptured." Ahmam feared Jiachang might call off the deal. She recalled the dwarf leaping clearly because when she was drawing it, her boyfriend at the time, Linzhan laughed at her, teasing her by saying she was doing a self-portrait. Ahmam, dainty and little when walking side by side with the lanky Linzhan was like a valley under a cliff. Linzhan rode a racing scooter at that time; Ahmam sometimes fell off of it but dared not complain. She often had bruised knees in those years. Recalling this, Ahmam felt indifferent now.

The memory stirred Jiachang, his cheeks turned crimson. "It was a miserable event; we only filled three rows in the entire student center. And our friends from class occupied two of the three rows.

You were so cynical; you said it was hard to find a high-class audience on a low-class campus, or something like that."

"That was then. Now my priority is to make more money. I am one of the top ten sales people in my company this month." Jiachang was a salesman for an American business, selling disposable contact lenses.

"Then buy these things as your prize." Ahmam said slowly.

"Shouldn't a prize be a new thing? I'd buy new things to reward myself." Jiachung replied still not 100 percent willing to buy the items.

"Then, forget about it." Ahmam said dryly to emphasize her point.

"I said if it weren't you…" Jiachang reckoned he should save Ahmam's pride, so he walked into her room without her invitation and started moving the things he had bought. He was tall, so while passing through the door, his head hit the decoration hanging over the doorframe. It was a bronze disc carved with two fishes and a jade pendant inscribed with a Buddhist scripture. On the corner, a golden sachet with tiger glands secretly emitted the fragrance of musk. Jiachang stood in front of the stereo; now his head hit the paper lantern, which was hung under the beam. The dark purple hibiscus on the lantern swayed before his eyes. "Always buying such useless stuff." He said as he shook his head.

He tried the remote control, in a flash sound started, accompanied by glistening blue-green lights on the panel. He picked up a CD randomly and pushed play. It was an old English song, "Goodbye Girl." Ahmam used to cry endlessly while listening to this song, the remake by a local singer had dulled the flavor of the original edition. The cheap reproduction of melancholy had unintentionally cured her broken heart.

Ahmam's room was the size of four tatamis, so when Jiachang lay down on the tatamis, she could only sit rigidly at one corner to avoid physical contact with him. "Are you still in touch with Linzhan?" he asked.

"No, we've not been in touch for a long time." Ahmam resented this question; she was sure that Jiachang knew the answer. Jiachang continued saying, "how strange, once so intimate and now totally disconnected." Ahmam sighed silently. He did not understand that in order to be totally disconnected from Linzhan, she had spent numerous nights crying. Ahmam's heart sank. She sighed not only because of the reminders of her past love, but also because she knew Jiachang had never really been in love. "What? Regret for the deal?" Jiachang sensed her change emotionally only he guessed wrong about why. To a person so insensitive and inexperienced, it was quite remarkable that he even noticed something.

"No, I don't need them," she replied. "Pick some CDs, too. My treat." Though her heart was leaden, she acted as carefree as possible. Seeing Jiachang rummage through her things so thoroughly, she realized that all the enjoyment of sounds and colors in the past would be gone; she was unable to keep them. As Jiachang tapped the touch-sensitive lamp with his feet along with the tempo, his stained white socks made Ahmam feel disgust for him, so she hurried him up. Jiachang began to take the wires apart and put the stereo in a box before moving it to his new Sentra.

"People might think we are burglars since we're moving things around at this time of day." Ahmam said looking around stealthily as she helped put the box into his car.

"Burglars wouldn't drive such a nice car." Jiachang replied confidently.

"It's not that good of a car." Ahmam shot back.

He started the car then got out to rub a mud stain off the roof with his bare hands. Not long ago Ahmam tried to borrow his car, but Jiachang was reluctant. He had said, "I can drive you wherever you want to go. Isn't it a better deal with a free chauffeur?" Ahmam knew he was afraid that she would crash his car. The senile soy pudding vendor always arrived at this lane at about ten in the morning, which was right as Jiachang drove his royal blue sedan away. As he drove past the vendor, some dust was stirred up, and Ahmam blinked her eyes. Seeing her property taken away, she shook her head and muttered, "Purchased like gold, sold like dirt." Her mother had warned her about the value drop of selling used goods.

Ahmam had started working right after school, one year and ten months earlier than Jiachang, while he served in the military. But now she was far behind the standard of living Taipei dwellers such as Jiachang enjoyed. Didn't she long for prosperity and fancy things? It was not that she had more noble goals that pulled her back from living a luxurious life; she was just a little unfortunate and very much incurably self-indulgent. When she left school, she devoted a lot of time to her relationships and only considered jobs that didn't require extra hours and had regular vacations. When she was single again, she felt that her career should be in the film industry. She didn't care about how much she could make. When her friend, "Eggy", who worked for a TV station bought a car with her annual bonus, Ahmam understood why her mother always called her naive.

When Ahmam returned upstairs, she heard the soy pudding vendor turn onto another street. Looking at the thin bunch of bills in her hand, she became lost in her reverie. Ahmam had once fancied buying a karaoke machine and putting it at the square in front of her family shrine. She'd host a reunion party and sing the lyrics to her favorite song in a vulgar but enticing style: "I ain't drunk, ain't drunk, please don't sympathize with a dancing girl." Ahmam was good at this style of singing. When she was younger, she had worked as a cashier for the nightclub her aunt ran. The club had a stage; all the singers were young girls dressed like butterflies, and they sang very seductive songs. The club manager heard Ahmam sing once without accompanying music and decided her performance carried the flavor they wanted for the stage, Ahmam was sent to get into costume. As soon as she was on the stage, Ahmam became a different person. She totally freaked out when she saw the lecherous faces of the customers; her mind went blank, and she forgot the lyrics. Her mother was disappointed; she said Ahmam was born without guts.

The little room looked so empty without the stereo. Anything valuable was seldom at Ahmam's disposal for a long time; it would usually switch to someone else's hands shortly after she bought them. She bought then sold, sold then bought.

Once when she was between jobs, she had to sell things as small as the lantern shade, some accessories she had made herself and items as big as her refrigerator. That time she was also determined to sell her favorite bone china, a whole set with cups and saucers. She priced the items, made fliers, and posted them on Shih-Da Road not far away from her place. On the fliers she wrote: "Used curios looking for new owners." Many students came in groups, but few transactions were made, Ahmam's roommates were bothered by the noisy visits. At last it was Tziyang that persuaded her new colleague from Hong Kong to check out Ahmam's stuff. That's how Ahmam met Juchi, another one of her boyfriends. Juchi was actually Tziyang's supervisor; he spoke a little Mandarin but couldn't read Chinese at all. Ahmam felt he had very similar features to a Hong Kong movie star, but what really attracted Ahmam to him was that he was a very quiet man. His quietness contradicted his good looks. The day he came with a bunch of friends to check out what Ahmam had to sell, they drank and ate like they were having a party. Ahmam was asked, playfully, where she kept the warranties for her things. They knew Ahmam bought things on a whim; she never kept any certificate, warranty, or manual. Nonetheless, she pretended to look for them. At one point Juchi said he'd buy anything the hostess was willing to sell. He spoke with strongly accented Mandarin. Everyone present was silent for a second trying to figure out what he meant. They suggested that Ahmam make the deal as profitable as possible. "She should consider selling herself at a good price," someone said in private.

Ahmam had not expected the sale to turn out this way. When she and Juchi set up a date to exchange money, she went elaborately dressed up. She dug out a suit buried in her closet and in order to get rid of the smell of mothballs, she borrowed Tziyang's Dior perfume. When the bus she took to meet Juchi got stuck in traffic. She almost passed out from her own perfume. When she arrived at the restaurant, she sat opposite Juchi. He shook his head, debating whether to say something. From his expression, Ahmam thought she had been tricked. She wondered if Juchi was going to cancel the deal. Why didn't he call her or have a word with Tziyang instead of humiliating her face to face? She was about to explode when Juchi said, "You look great today but that outfit is not you." He said the first time he saw Ahmam, he thought her smile was like that of a Barbie doll's. That's how Ahmam found out Juchi was the representative for an international toy supplier. That night she got a lot more money for the deal than they had originally agreed to and she started leading the resplendent lifestyle that Juchi offered her. Their relationship had lasted until the past October. It was exactly the time for the once-blooming roses to become entirely dried specimens.

Despite having no income, Ahmam hardly restrained herself from shopping for things. She knew her good looks qualified her to be a mistress, and her character didn't qualify her for much else. She was not spending extravagantly; she just didn't know how to say no. All that was left now from what she had procured with the credit card Juchi applied for in her name was a whole set of encyclopedias standing by the wall. Unfortunately these encyclopedias couldn't answer most of her doubts about life, she had only read several pages of books B and G. Ahmam had bought the encyclopedias while sitting in a fast food restaurant, waiting for Juchi to pick her up. They were going to a movie. A girl approached and asked her if she could share the table. Ahmam nodded, saying "sure" without even thinking about it. Her response cost Juchi nearly forty thousand dollars.

On their way to the cinema, Ahmam told Juchi she had just bought a set of encyclopedias. Juchi did not ask how much she paid he simply asked, "Do you really need it?"

She said: "The girl hadn't made a sale for a whole day!" Juchi did not say anything more. After the movie, he took her to eat oyster noodles at a stand; they had never eaten at a food stand before. After that day, Juchi rarely called Ahmam. Later she learned from Tziyang that Juchi had applied for a position back in Hong Kong and gone back there. This short-lived romance was so ethereal to Ahmam; nonetheless, the things she bought with Juchi's money were packed in her place, and their smells were so real. Ahmam knew that her relationship with Juchi wouldn't last but did not expect it to end so fast. She felt like part of her had been amputated, but the pain of the wound was much less than the frightening sensation of the void. Her friends said she did not deserve a wealthy life: "The fat meat was already on your chop sticks and you dropped it," they said. Ahmam especially missed Juchi's cantonese-accented mandarin. The absurd misunderstanding of a question such as "How old are you?" was confused with "bathing water" before they learned to understand each other.

After breaking up with Juchi, Ahmam would often suddenly be roused from sleep. Looking at the veil of night, she'd unconsciously stretch her hand inside her top to feel the scar on her back. The scar was a souvenir of their lovemaking on a new carpet. Juchi's knees were also scraped that time. Now Ahmam appreciated that there was something left for each of them for the rest of their lives. Juchi usually turned up at her house after the dinner parties and events he held for his clients.

Ahmam did not pull herself together until she figured out what had happened. The first action she took was to bring the credit card Juchi had given her to a dilapidated park in front of her place and bury it. A couple of old men stared at her mindlessly. Second, she went to check out job listings in newspapers. Ahmam reckoned she should not find a mentally challenging job. After all, her broken heart was not healed yet. She picked what looked like a waitress job at a place with an elegant name. The interview took her to a place several kilometers from her home. She walked past the yard decorated with false rocks that were lit by green neon and found herself standing in a lobby furnished with leather sofas. The man interviewing her gestured for her to sit down and asked her how old she was. "Twenty-nine," she replied and glanced at the man. The man was surprised by her answer; he began to scrutinize her closely. Ahmam wondered whether he felt she was too old or too young. He explained the shifts and told her the base pay was thirty thousand. "Great, thirty thousand, but what do I do?" she wondered. Suddenly, the man hit a button and a door opened up. A woman wearing a tight dress led her inside. Ahmam suddenly realized that she was in an underground casino, by each gambling table was a girl leaning against a gambler. No one bothered to check out who the visitor was. Ahmam over heard a man telling a girl that she could make more money by getting laid. Ahmam turned to leave but couldn't find the exit. In the dimly lit casino, Ahmam felt everyone's gaze piercing her flesh. Once the girl showing her around she realized how ill at ease Ahmam was, she pressed the remote control in her hand and the door opened. Ahmam explained to the man that it wasn't the kind of job she was applying for before escaping the place. Even though she intended to find a job that was not mentally challenging, she did not plan to sell her body.

When Ahmam went down the road again later, the underground casino was gone. The dreamy air reminded her of Juchi. Ahmam started to worry that the man who had interviewed her might be in jail now, cursing her because he assumed she reported his illegal business, even though she hadn't. As the year dragged to an end, fewer people quit, thus fewer jobs became available. Ahmam became indolent again. Every day she walked around like a ghost. If it was not raining, she'd walk to the market with her oversized slippers around noontime. Once she bought a basket for her bathroom. She realized she did not know how to nail it into the wall. She asked the vendor, who replied, "Let your husband do it for you!"

"Husband? Is there a temporary husband for rent service? Do I look like a married woman?" Ahmam wondered as she finally hammered four nails into the tiled wall. She had to face the fact that without a job, she was not only disconnected from the world but also from herself. Ahmam recalled when she was in second grade, she fell from a two-story high breadfruit tree to everyone's surprise she was not injured. She learned from the experience that in life one should have great resilience.

Ahmam finally got a part-time job as a voice actor through an introduction from Tziyang. She only worked when they could not find enough other voices; most of the films Ahmam worked on were adult videos. She found it hard to mimic the actresses' murmurs, not unlike melted butter and their sexy moaning. It was around this time, Xufang was getting married. Xufang gave her roommates her white cat, Mimi, who happened to be in heat and made seductive cries every now and then. Ahmam, accompanied by her roommates, started leaning against their apartment wall stealthily watching the adult channel as their neighbors watched late at night. That's how Ahmam learned to handle the job.

Ahmam knew nothing about the technical issues regarding the filming of these adult videos. She was glad that the dubbing was recorded on a single track, and then the voices of the men and women would be mixed in the lab. The engineer often dozed off while she was working, so Ahmam was essentially alone in the studio lit by the fluorescent tube, facing the phallus-like microphone and uttering nasal sounds according to the movements shown on the screen. A cup of green tea, strong and yellowish, was provided in case the voice actor was thirsty. The money she made for dubbing barely paid her rent and transportation to the recording lab.

One day, Ahmam noticed that a new chain restaurant in her neighborhood had hung up a red banner saying they were recruiting people belonging to the "New Generation." Ahmam was the oldest among the "New Generation," she pretended to be a customer first. She had a chance to ask as casually as possible, "Do you hire people who are not "New Generation'?" The maître de said politely it was just a slogan; they didn't mind hiring people of all ages. Ahmam turned her application in right there, the maître de inquired whether she could start as soon as possible and she transitioned to an employee almost immediately. On her first day, her task was giving coffee refills to customers. The job paid her sixty-five dollars an hour and she had to wear a very stupid apron. From time to time, the maître de would remind her of things like: "Your apron is inside out. Hold the round plate with one hand. Forks should be put under the letter *S* printed on the table tissue. Don't mix up the A set, B set, or C set menus. Don't deliver bread to customers ordering rice. Remember to bring the big white spoon for customers ordering mushroom porridge. Look carefully: vegetable noodle and Italian style pasta are different. One is green, and one is yellow!"

During her first few weeks, Ahmam felt ill at ease mixing with co-workers who were still in school; the only thing she said was "Welcome!" to customers. Watching her always coming and going in a hurry, the chef once asked whether she was taking preparation classes for college entrance examinations. Ahmam smiled but didn't answer. A woman joined the team who was going through a divorce. She wished to learn how to make a living on her own. "Pre-divorce occupational training," she called it. Ahmam finally had someone to chat with. Sometimes when the woman couldn't make it to work, Ahmam would take her shift or she would give the woman a hand when she was assigned to cleaning the bathroom

In the mornings, a well-known film director who had strongly denied having an extramarital affair often dined at the restaurant with a lady friend. He invariably wore a pair of sunglasses and ordered from the A set menu. Ahmam thought if she were several years younger, she might leave the plates behind and boldly ask the director to hire her, saying she'd be willing to work any trivial job. But now she felt she was too old to be so audacious. When she confided in a co-worker, a large college girl with very short hair, she felt little sympathy in her response: "You must be much older than me. No New Generation and a Cancer?" The college girl left her alone as soon as she came to this conclusion. She turned to the door, shouting, "Welcome!" to the arriving guests with an unnaturally shrill voice, the maître de, who was also several years younger than Ahmam smiled at the girl encouragingly.

Almost every day at noon, a fat old woman, obviously a pensioner, would have lunch; she always ordered from the B set menu. She insisted on using straws with red stripes for her drink. One time all the red straws were gone, she did not want to use any other color, so Ahmam was sent to find red straws. She walked to shops on street after street in vain and returned without a red straw. The stubbornness of the fat old woman was amazing; she left, refusing to eat.

About one month after that incident, Ahmam spilled a sundae in a goblet on the hip of a filthy old man. The maître de freaked out and immediately asked Ahmam to clean up the man's pants. Ahmam refused; she claimed that the man tripped her. She forgot the restaurant trained its staff in the style of Japanese corporations: customers must be always right. Ahmam quit, she regretted only that she would no longer get the free bread the restaurant offered employees after closing each night. Yindang declared they should never dine at the place, and all the roommates agreed. After some time had passed, they went back and ordered take-out bread when Ahmam was not around.

Juchi came to Ahmam's mind again because she was having such a problem making a living. Juchi was like a spider, Ahmam thought; he went to weave his web. Cuddling, playing puppies with their innocent smiles made Ahmam think of Juchi with a dull ache. Fires also reminded her of Juchi. Strangely enough, they had seen fires together a few times when they strolled the local streets. "I seldom saw such dramatic scenes in Hong Kong. Life and death are so close here," Juchi once said to her while touching her hand tenderly.

Tziyang

Tziyang had attached a one-thousand-dollar bill to a note on her door asking Ahmam to buy two potted plants for her. The door was blackish green; Tziyang had painted it before she went back to her hometown for the New Year holidays. The color reminded Ahmam of the small township offices back home. In the note, Tziyang thanked Ahmam and praised her taste, saying she knew Ahmam would select two wonderful, auspicious plants for her and she also mentioned how crucial it was because the plants might change her life.

Beside the note, a picture of Tziyang smiled lovingly. Only four teeth were showing, in order to maintain the sense of modesty women were supposed to have. Ahmam was amused. Tziyang wished to get married so badly, she'd follow any instruction in feng shui that might help her to find a husband. "What a lazy woman." Ahmam said, but her tone was much more caring than her words.

The sudden, impatient honking of cars broke the silence. Ahmam ran to the balcony to find out what was going on, she saw that the intersection below was totally jammed. The cars were lined-up, not moving at all, conjured a picture of an octopus in her mind. When she ran downstairs, she found a well-dressed girl lying in the road. Ahmam couldn't see her face; she did see the tires of an overturned scooter beside her were still rotating. No one, including the girl and all the spectators, moved. Finally a truck driver approached and bent over the girl to check her, then yelled, "Not dead, don't worry!" His thundering shout roused the girl, and she came back to consciousness. The traffic flow did not improve until an ambulance picked the girl up and sped away with a shrill siren. Ahmam, now feeling lost, walked toward the florist two streets away. As she walked, she was lost in her thoughts. She knew it was her weakness to be so easily stirred up emotionally, especially by haunting images.

Before arriving at the florist, she stopped by a boutique to check on whether the Louie Vuitton purse she had left there to be sold had been purchased. Ahmam was disappointed to find it was still there. Ahmam knew the boutique proprietress because she had shopped for outfits there a couple of times, at first the proprietress did not want to put the purse in her store. "Why not?" Ahmam asked. "It's real Louie Vuitton. If it's sold, you can have a commission."

"I don't want it *because* it's real. Ahmam, in this neighborhood, no one can really afford genuine Louie Vuitton. Shoppers would be satisfied with fake ones." Ahmam now understood how expensive the present Juchi had given her was. She touched the purse, which she had only used twice, with regret. But she lifted her face, determined and implored the proprietress to sell it for her. She offered 40 percent of the transaction as commission. The proprietress said yes immediately; she must have thought Ahmam was foolish.

There was no cash since it wasn't sold, Ahmam turned away gloomily.

The shocking images eventually faded a little when Ahmam arrived at the florist. She saw blooming red flowers with vibrant green leaves. There were not many shoppers and the phone never stopped ringing. Ahmam waited. The florist was a woman with straight hair that was neatly cut around her ears. Today she wore a Chinese-styled bright red cotton jacket. Looking at her through the store window, Ahmam could feel the beauty in the woman's spirit, standing beside the flowers she supplied—a combination of firmness and tenderness.

Some shoppers stopped but left without buying anything. Ahmam decided not to hurry. She took time appreciating and looking at the plants for Tziyang. She noticed a pot sitting on the shelf at about eye level blooming and another plant, which hung under an iron frame, Ahmam thought both were striking. Ahmam selected them for Tziyang. She picked up some winter plums and some gingko flowers for her own jar. As the florist came near her, her bright red jacket made all the colors of the flowers fade in a second. Ahmam smelled the light smoke of a menthol cigarette.

As the florist was packaging up Ahmam's purchase, a woman, about sixty years old came in and nimbly picked some scarlet flowers from a water basin. Ahmam knew older people liked bright colors because their eyesight had degenerated. Ahmam admired the flowers and gestured for the florist to go ahead and help the old woman first. The old woman bade her to use red wrapping paper that was as bright as possible. She explained, "Someone downstairs from our home died and the mourning family did not hang up red couplet papers for the neighbors."

"Don't get upset," the florist said. "The difference between a living man and a dead man is that one is still breathing while the other one stops. That's all; it's nothing." The old woman shut her mouth; she must have felt embarrassed that even at her age, her fears about death were still so intense.

Ahmam watched the old woman leave with the red flowers. The faded vitality of life and the blooming charm created a contrast. The florist gazed at Ahmam and inquired, "You are not married, are you?" Ahmam smiled, shaking her head. She bent toward the lilies to smell the light fragrance they emitted. The jade pendent of Pisces she wore on her neck dangled.

"May I introduce you to someone? A friend's son, he is thirty-something or forty. He has inherited three houses and said he doesn't care if his wife is plain." She thought of something and added, "But you are not a plain girl. You are pretty."

Ahmam felt funny. Thirty-something or forty was a big range. She had met many people who wanted to introduce her to someone recently. Even when she was shopping for clothes at a street stand, the young female vendor suggested introducing her brother to Ahmam.

"What's your name?"

"Wu Chun-Mam." which was Ahmam's family name.

Ahmam saw the florist write down the phonetic forms of her name on the ordering paper, but she spelled it wrong. Ahmam recalled the first time she saw her name. It was on the rice vat and the bamboo door of their adobe house. *Mam* meant "full," and *Chun* meant "spring," Her mother liked to attach red couplets for New Year's Day with these characters. When Ahmam was in elementary school, she sometimes saw "Chun" attached upside down over the maroon ceramic vat. As she grew older, Ahmam realized the upside down Chun meant the arrival of spring, and this character had been with her throughout every occasion she had ever been through but her mother made mistakes a lot. She once attached Mam at the door of Ahmam's big brother, and she once absurdly attached it to their bathroom. Ahmam suspected that her mother did not read at all. She remembered when her mother moved the stool around with a pile of the red papers and climbed up and down to find places for them. After she glued each paper, she'd put her palms together for several seconds. Her pious attitude in praying was like a different person from the one that scolded her husband violently. Ahmam guessed her mother must have memorized those characters according to the number of strokes. She cared about such trivial things very much because she knew they might be significant in feng shui.

Once she considered changing Ahmam's name because their family name Wu sounded the same as "nothing," thus no matter which auspicious characters followed it, it ended up being nothing. She blamed her husband's family name for their daughter earning nothing financially and there being nothing for her marriage.

Ahmam's mother agreed with the family name only once. The time a street storyteller told the story of General Wu San-Kuei from the Ming Dynasty; her mother did not listen to the ending and assumed since Wu San-Kuei was a general, Wu must be a good name. How can a family with the same name of a general not to be blessed? Later she saw a Taiwanese opera and realized that Wu San-Kuei was not really a good person, she was convinced that her daughter's name must be changed. She consulted Ahmam's uncle, a policeman, asking him to check if there was anyone in the county using the same name so they would have a strong reason to change Ahmam's name. But Ahmam was unwilling to change her name; to her, a changed name meant a changed past. She went to her uncle and told him she had no intention of having a different name. It saved her uncle a lot of trouble, so he told Ahmam's mother that Wu Chun-Mam was a unique name.

The florist finally finished the elaborate wrapping style she insisted on, and the two potted plants looked like the gaudy decorations in the lobby of some securities company, seemingly about to devour visitors with their overly shining red and golden wrappings. The florist also warmheartedly said she should deliver the plants to Ahmam's home, so she called her son, who was playing computer games next door, to be in charge of the store while she was away.

The florist put the two pots on the front seat of her motorcycle, and Ahmam squeezed herself on the rear seat, behind the overweight florist. The bright red woman drove past several lanes and stopped at a vendor of couplet papers without consulting Ahmam. "Fumi! How's the business?" she asked the owner. She got up from her motorcycle and picked some of the couplets with an easy manner.

"So-so. I am about to put things away and go home; all those who need couplets have bought them already, young couples never care to hang up such outdated things."

The florist set eyes on the baby on the vendor's chest and said, "This baby will be a good reader and learner in the future." Ahmam wondered how she was able to tell the fortune of a baby who was still in swaddling clothes. Ahmam browsed the couplets after the florist. The ancient flavor contained in the calligraphic strokes was reduced, but the tradition inherited from Chinese culture was still there. While appreciating the writing, Ahmam's mind began splattering, like ink dropping on Indian paper.

In the winter break of Ahmam's third year in college, the prices of agricultural products were lower than the farmer's costs. Farming became a tiring and worthless business; villagers felt their lives were worse than those of cattle. After criticizing the government for doing nothing and cursing the officials for sucking people's blood, Ahmam's mother decided to sell couplet papers. She walked a long distance to the town and bought a lot of them from a wholesaler.

This happened right after the first time Ahmam and Linzhan broke up; Ahmam felt the winter break was especially long and harsh. In contrast, her mother, with the mentality of a tiger, was ready to fight. She was eager to teach Ahmam how to do business. "You pose like this and yell as loud as possible. Remember, you must say your products are the cheapest and once a passerby stops to check your stuff, others will follow. The more people get around your stand, the more chances you have to make deals. People are all the same: they follow what others do." Ahmam's mother kept instructing her until the last moment before she set out. In the bustling market, Ahmam forced herself to speak in a weak, irresolute voice, announcing, "Ten red envelopes for five dollars only. Ten red envelopes for five dollars only..." She was far from yelling. Some shoppers did stop by to check out her things, but they were more interested in reading through the couplet papers than the price she was offering, and Ahmam was most afraid of the housewives who compared prices of several places.

They'd frown at hearing the prices of the couplet papers and complain. "Too expensive, too expensive..." As they grumbled, they never stopped flipping the papers; the red papers tied by thin threads were wearing out quickly from the relentless fingering.

Some nasty old men liked to give her a hard time by asking teasingly, "Miss, how much is this?" Ahmam did not really hate them even though they smiled at her with horribly stained teeth and carved wrinkles. She just wished that the New Year holidays would pass as quickly as possible. At the end of the day, Ahmam's sales at the busiest spot of the market were far less satisfactory than her mother's, who had to set up her stand out of the way of the shoppers. The next day Ahmam's father was assigned by her mother to aid Ahmam, at least to make her more courageous. Once her mother walked away, her father said: "You take care of the business first; Daddy is going to have breakfast." The breakfast took him the whole day; he never came back. Thanks to Ahmam's elementary school classmate Laihung, Ahmam had one day's good business at last. Laihung matured faster than her peers; she was like a young adult when she was a teenager and got married right after she finished junior high school. Her husband was an ungainly boy from a well-to-do family; the marriage assured her a carefree lifestyle. Laihung dragged many of her relatives to buy couplet papers from Ahmam, and Ahmam thanked her again and again. Laihung invariably introduced Ahmam to her relatives, saying, "We went to the same elementary school and she was a model student. She always got top marks; that's what her name means, full marks!" Ahmam and her father failed to sell very many couplet papers, so they hung them at their own home for many years to follow. The words were all the same, but fresh red ones replaced the faded ones.

Looking at those red papers, Ahmam was reminded of her father, and tears brimmed from her eyes. The florist glanced at her and was bewildered but did not think more about it. She quickly picked some couplet papers, and when Fumi offered a discount that saved her change, the florist insisted on paying the full price. They spent several moments longer until the florist accepted the favor. Before she got on her scooter, the florist pinched the baby and looked satisfied when it started crying. After two streets, Ahmam gave the florist directions and they arrived at the lane of Ahmam's place. Ahmam told her where she lived and the florist lifted her head to look at the out stretched structure over the roof. Ahmam seemed to see images of clouds flit over her eyes. The florist said in a sentimental tone, "Girl, you should find someone and settle down with him." Ahmam thanked her. She did not want to worry a stranger about her status.

The florist laughed amiably and wished Ahmam the best before switching on her scooter, she turned and asked eagerly with strongly accented Mandarin, "You don't have boyfriend, do you?" Ahmam was turning the door key of the building, but she smiled at her and shook her head. The florist seemed determined. She must have some idea in mind. She patted her own voluptuous chest and said: "I will contact you... people call me Mrs. Kao. What's your number?" She carefully wrote down Ahmam's number and before riding away, she added, "I hope you will find a good husband in the New Year. "Such passionate people are fewer and fewer nowadays," Ahmam thought, watching the bright red profile disappear in the haze.

Ahmam put the blooming potted plants on Tziyang's sunlit balcony as she had asked earlier. Ahmam was told they were quite easy to take care of. Tziyang got the idea from a fortune-teller, who said that with flowers, her luck in the New Year would be especially good. Tziyang made a wish to be married in the New Year; she had also attached a painting of a pair of chickens looking at each other affectionately to her door. But Tziyang did not notice or did not know that both chickens were cocks. Ahmam figured she'd better not to tell Tziyang, or she would go crazy. Tziyang had moved back to Taiwan from America the previous year; she said she finally saw reality that it was hopeless for her to hang on to the States. Tziyang also knew that in the small community of Chinese, she wouldn't find a man, or she wouldn't find a man without suffering. Ahmam, among other roommates, could relate to how Tziyang felt. Tziyang had actively participated in all kinds of matchmaking events since she returned to Taiwan, but she had found no one yet. Tziyang hated to attend the parties of her peers; everyone couldn't help but show off their education, occupational titles, and achievements.

That's why Ahmam, unsophisticated and without any shining title, became Tziyang's closest friend. Tziyang had a most impossible accident during one of her blind dates. The matchmaker was unable to make it, so Tziyang and the man she was meeting had set up the time and place for the date at a cafe. That evening Tziyang went to the laundry service not far from their home to pick up the dress she sent to be dry-cleaned. She returned empty handed and outraged. She complained, "Shit, it's not done yet. I told the guy what I was going to wear today."

"I thought you sent it to the laundry service a week ago. How come it's not done yet?"

"Exactly! I shouted at the laundryman and accused him of destroying my potential happiness."

"Look on the bright side: you can observe the man before identifying yourself."

"Maybe he thinks the same thing. Besides, the dress is my lucky dress. I need it tonight."

Ahmam burst out laughing.

"I am serious! I wore it for my masters' thesis oral defense, and got a high pass even with my not-so-fluent English. Wasn't it lucky?"

Tziyang finally made up her mind about what to wear by six o'clock. It was a long dress with layers of ornate lace, reminiscent of those English court ladies. After she put on high heel shoes, her slim profile made her look like she was walking on stilts. She chose a clutch decorated with fake pearls. She walked over to Ahmam, saying with her bloody red lips, "To conquer or die. Read some scriptures and pray for the Buddha to help me."

Even before Ahmam started her prayer, while the air still smelled of Tziyang's intoxicating perfume, she got a call asking if Tziyang lived there. Ahmam thought it was Tziyang's date and wondered why he was so impatient. But to Ahmam's surprise, the caller said Tziyang was in the hospital. Ahmam and Yingdan hurried into the hospital, emergency room. Tziyang was done getting her wounds dressed, but her face was purple with anger. "He is the one who should be blamed..." Not knowing how to explain what had happened, Tziyang simply muttered, "The taxi driver." She pointed at a man standing in a corner of the ward. He looked apologetic. Ahmam and Yingdan were convinced it must be this man's fault, but they he didn't look like a taxi driver. They thought Tziyang was confused by the injury to her head.

The man then explained that it was his first day being a taxi driver, and he caused the accident and hurt Tziyang before making any money.

"Never mind. It's our fate to know each other in this way." Yingdan spoke instinctively. But her effort at mediating only earned her a solid kick from the still-angry Tziyang. Tziyang's date was ruined, but it unintentionally opened a door for Yingdan.

Not long after the ending of the bitter sandwich romance, Yingdan fell in love with the taxi driver. Ahmam gave him the nickname Tchaikovscabi.

If Tchaikovscabi was short on money, Yingdan would bring him food or suggest where they could go for fun. Tchaikovscabi once complained that his car consumed too much gas, all Yingdan's roommates believed that Yingdan should lose some weight. They worried that she might lose another boyfriend because of food, and even though she did not care about her weight, they thought she really should consider the risk of growing bigger than the car door.

As soon as she recovered from her injury, Tziyang dragged Ahmam to a party on Christmas Eve that was specifically for single men and women. Tziyang was the only one dressed up formally and she had been sitting all night. Ahmam remembered that she stuck to her chair until the party was over. Tziyang did not expect that there would be a lot of games going on and the lights would be turned bright and dark alternately, because of her formal outfit, no one dared to invite her to play.

On their way home, a chilly winter wind blew over Tziyang's naked shoulders, her face was red with annoyance as she said, "In America, people attend such parties formally. Why do we not dress up here?" Ahmam had no idea what the parties in America were like, but she fully understood Tziyang's embarrassment. The men were outnumbered by women, playing games were the only way for these singles to have interactions and get to know each other. In a party like that, everything they saw was superficial. Tziyang and Ahmam decided they could benefit from attending such events.

As Tziyang's annoyance faded, the two women walked in silence. Motorcycles howled by, heading for late-night craziness. People murmured good-byes after gatherings and lovers cuddled. Quite a few people hung out, none were as uneasy as Ahmam and Tziyang. As they listened to the staccato of Tziyang's clicking high heels, Tziyang finally sighed deeply, which turned foggy in the air. She stretched out to hold Ahmam's icy hand, smiling brightly. Ahmam knew Tziyang's horoscope belonged to an earth sign, once she decided to settle down, she would be like tree roots touching the earth, solidly gripping the soil and following the principles and goals of life. Not surprisingly, Tziyang had gone to a fortune-teller and was told she was destined to gain nothing in this year. Tziyang began to expect the coming of the New Year and stopped going out before it. Ahmam followed Tziyang, entering into hibernation too. At night, they often draped a coat over their shoulders and cooked soup in the murky, narrow kitchen. They'd leave the dishes till the next meal when they needed clean dishes again. The oil congealing on the surface of water was like the life of the two women, weightless and powerless.

On weekend afternoons, if it was not too cold, they'd sit on the rattan chairs on the balcony, holding Mimi the cat. Behind the drawn-up silky blue drape, they were like those old women in nursing homes. Sunlight tenderly lit their faces and the still-vigorous youth bizarrely mixed with an image of two elderly figures. They poured hot tea into white porcelain cups on the small tea table, as each girl fell into her own reverie. Ahmam recollected a certain date with Juchi, when they sat together in a pub, looking out over the ocean at boats in the mist. Each sip of the hot tea made her regret her sincere but mindless romance.

She had often felt the need to go to the bathroom during their meals. Her stirring belly made sweat beads ooze from her forehead. Ahmam did not know if it was because of the food or because of her uneasiness. Embarrassed, she told Juchi she had to go to bathroom, and Juchi looked at her with amusement and said, "Go ahead, Barbie."

One time Juchi got a haircut, and the bangs over his forehead made him look like a comedian. Ahmam burst out laughing. Juchi could feel the affection in her laughter, like a warm wind gusts from the south. Her relationship with Juchi brought her opportunities to go to every high-end restaurant in Taipei. She had tried all kinds of extravagant cuisine. They traveled to Yilan one time by train and even in the countryside they managed to find a charming place for coffee. Juchi was going back to Hong Kong the next day, Ahmam thought of her mother having asked for an ointment for insect bites that was produced in Hong Kong. She reminded Juchi to buy some for her, Juchi said lovingly, "of course. I will find anything you want."

When Juchi returned from Hong Kong, he brought a blue-checkered Polo bag stuffed with various bottles of drugs that Yindang asked for and a dozen types of the ointment Ahmam's mother wanted. They were packed with white, light green and orange labels in different sized glass jars. When Ahmam gave them to her mother, she questioned if they were fake and nagged Ahmam about being wasteful.

"They were bought by a local; they can't be fake." Ahmam said defending Juchi.

"Since when do you have friends from Hong Kong?" She took them under the light and scrutinized the labels carefully before twisting open one of the jars. She scraped a little ointment with her finger to spread over her neck and asked Ahmam to massage her shoulders. The mint flavor in the air temporarily relieved the tension between the mother and daughter. The Polo bag didn't impress Ahmam; she sold it to a friend for a decent price. Juchi did not say anything when he learned about it. The white teacups from which Ahmam drank tea with Tziyang in the winter afternoons were purchased after Ahmam broke up with Juchi. At that time she had suddenly become obsessed with pure white tea sets but could no longer afford them.

Ahmam waited until the set was on sale, Tziyang used her credit card to buy it for Ahmam so she would be able to pay her for it in installments.

As the two women lingered on their own thoughts, the bright lights of the subway construction nearby unexpectedly switched on. In the winter fog, their facial contours were clearly outlined and their memories were enlivened. Looking at their own faces partially reflected by the tea in the cups, they aged fast when wind gusts wrinkled the surface. The mirrored image saddened Ahmam, who had loved paired things all her life. She sighed and said to Tziyang, "no human being can really be coupled except by his or her own double."

One night, while Ahmam lay in bed, tears flowed from her eyes from a memory. Ahmam recalled how many years ago, when Linzhan made love to her, she was in the same position. After their lovemaking, Linzhan cried in front of her for the first time. Ahmam was confused; they were just having fun and even arguing about who should be on the top. Ahmam suggested she should be on the top so Linzhan could save his energy, Linzhan said, "I am so rich; my energy will never run out." He turned her over. Linzhan ejaculated, then collapsed. "What happened? Rich guy defeated by inflation?" Ahmam teased. To her surprise, Linzhan's tears gushed, he said gloomily, "I have walked through the valley of the shadow of death."

Lihsiang

Watching Ahmam at a distance with a huge totoro, one might have mistaken her for a little girl. Looking at her more closely, one could see that her eyes were filled with gloominess, her eyelashes blinked along with the wavy fur of the totoro in the wind.

Ahmam lifted her head and saw a neon sign at a department store advertising sales. She thought of the two coupons Tziyang gave her, she also knew that even with discounts she couldn't afford anything in there.

About one month ago, around winter solstice, Ahmam had accompanied Tziyang on quite a cold day to shop at the department store. Tziyang's plan was to buy two outfits with a budget of about four thousand dollars, the department store was giving out raffle tickets for every three thousand dollars spent. Tziyang won more discounts from the raffle, so she decided to buy more. As she bought more, she won more. Tziyang realized such a gimmick was meant to encourage unstoppable shopping but she was completely overwhelmed. Tziyang couldn't wait until they got home to put on one of the coats she had just purchased but was outraged when a chunky girl with exactly the same style and color of the coat got on the bus. Tziyang immediately took her coat off and passed it to Ahmam. Ahmam thought, "The price of being unique is high!" That was the coat Ahmam was wearing now, strangely enough, it looked even more expensive on Ahmam than it had on Tziyang.

Ahmam's memory of shopping during her first year in senior high school was bittersweet. She and Ahchih had browsed in an upscale store; Ahmam spotted a sweater and mistook the four-digit number on the price tag for a three-digit price. She told the saleswoman she wanted two of them and did not realized she couldn't afford them at all until the sweaters were packed. Ahmam apologized to the saleswoman, but she snobbishly said, "Don't look around if you can't afford it!" Ahchih rushed over when she heard the hurtful words of the saleswoman. She threw a bunch of money in the woman's face. Ahmam wore the sweaters for a long time. The more worn out the sweaters were, the more she cherished her friendship with Ahchih, especially when everything in life was short-lived like flowers and smoke.

Ahmam thought of Lihsiang. She checked the time and decided to walk toward a boutique not faraway to see her. She was her older brother's ex-girlfriend from several years ago. The boutique was on the second floor. Lihsiang was about to close the iron door when Ahmam arrived. Watching Ahmam approach, Lihsiang did not say hi instead she measured her up. She opened the iron door again and told Ahmam she had two suits that might be her size. The two women dug for the suits in a store that was so small it hardly had enough room for two people to turn around at the same time.

They found them. With the bag of two suits and the huge totoro in hand, Ahmam followed Lihsiang to her place. At the intersection, Ahmam hurried to get across when she saw the green light but Lihsiang pulled her back, saying, "I don't feel comfortable if I don't know how long the green light will last. It makes me feel so insecure when I think the light might turn red when I'm halfway across." They did not go until the light turned red and then green again. Ahmam now had a better idea why Lihsiang had to leave her brother. His research work in the forest did not give her a strong sense of security. While they were waiting for the traffic light, Ahmam suggested they count how many units there were in an incomplete development across the intersection. The buildings were never completed due to an ownership dispute, thus the grid like structure was exposed. "Thirteen floors, each floor has twenty-two units, so there were two hundred and fifty-six units…" The two women lifted their heads, concentrating on their calculations. Some people followed their gazes; looking up to check out what had attracted their attention. When they finally walked across the intersection, they decided to go up in the building. In the empty floors without facades, the women must have looked like two moving black dots in the eyes of the passing drivers. Sometimes they moved faster, sometimes slower.

When the large clock hanging over the next building struck 2:00 p.m., they climbed to the top floor. With their hair being blown around crazily by gusty wind, the two women became excited. They screamed toward the ground far below them, all the sounds in a busy city cut off their screams; everything down there still acted on its own rhythm. They got tired and leaned against a concrete wall. The climbing made them sweat; they felt the heavy grease and dust of the city actually dripping away in their perspiration.

"Ahmam, you have not changed at all," Lihsiang said breathlessly.

Ahmam laughed. She pointed to the sky and said, "It's God's will." Lihsiang shook her head and laughed.

The sky seemed clearer when seen from a higher floor. Ahmam deliberately put the totoro on the ledge of the building, asking, "Will he die if he falls from this high?"

"A stuffed toy doesn't die." Lihsiang realized how stupid they were being now; she suggested they should go back down.

When they reached the ground level again, Ahmam felt like she was floating. She now understood that the feeling of lightness must be experienced through heaviness. Lightness wouldn't be significant without heaviness. The sky began to turn clearer.

They made their way to Lihsiang's apartment. When they arrived Lihsiang's roommate was not in the living room but she had left the TV blaring on MTV. On the screen, a woman wearing jeans lay somewhere, a pair of masculine, dark hands were unbuttoning her jeans. Tomomi, a Japanese girl, walked out of her bedroom. She was eighteen years old; she came to Taiwan without speaking any Chinese. She was lucky that Lihsiang shared her apartment with her; this saved her a lot of trouble.

"Hello, good afternoon," she said to Ahmam and Lihsiang as she entered the room.

The way Tomomi said good afternoon in Chinese sounded like "having husband" in Taiwanese. She smiled as she opened the screen door to the balcony where she was doing laundry. She sang a Japanese song along with the rhythm of the splashing water. The melody had been made into a Chinese song called "Loving You for Another Ten Thousand Years." Ahmam was very familiar with it. Tomomi's singing immediately brought an air of those cheap parties where girls performed with garish outfits and thick makeup. The screen door creaked open again. It was Ren Chunlang entering, another roommate of Lihsiang. Her family name, Ren, meant "cold" and her first name meant, "Spring orchard." She was indeed like a cold orchard sketched on a white paper, near forty, the paper had started to wrinkle. Her face and body revealed that she must be about a generation older than Lihsiang.

"You aren't going home for New Year?" Lihsiang asked Chunlang.

"I am leaving in a moment. Chen Tailan is picking me up. We are bringing my mattress back." Chunlang patted her shoulder; it must have been sore because of the cleaning and washing work she had done earlier.

"You don't have a mattress at home?"

"No," Chunlang answered in a matter-of-fact tone. She went on to explain in a toneless voice that she fell from a motorcycle not long ago and her backbone had been injured. She wanted to bring the mattress because she'd need something softer to sleep on than the wooden bed at home.

"Why not just buy one at her hometown?" both Ahmam and Lihsiang wondered but said nothing.

As Chunlang lifted her top and showed them a large bruise that looked like a cut-open taro, Chen Tailan arrived. Chen Tailan was a man in his early thirties, obviously much younger than Chunlang. His dark face turned to the girls and he smiled shyly toward them before quickly walking into Chunlang's bedroom. He seemed to have made himself at home. When he emerged again, he had lifted Chunlang's mattress up over his head. Ahmam and Lihsiang approached to offer help, but Chunlang told them, "He is okay. He is used to moving things." Chunlang followed him downstairs, and Lihsiang and Ahmam went to the balcony to watch them leave.

"Happy New Year!"

"Here's wishing we all find our Mr. Right in the New Year!"

People smiled at their wishes to each other or shook their heads at the boldness of girls nowadays, so Lihsiang yelled happily after them for a few moments longer as they left. Not long after their departure, Chunlang returned, panting from running up the stairs. She said she forgot something and rushed to the kitchen to fetch a bag of vegetables. Lihsiang and Ahmam looked at each other and laughed.

Lihsiang said: "that woman is so forgetful."

Chunlang reminded Ahmam of those traditional women who brought chickens with them on buses as gifts to their relatives living far away. They watched the pickup leave again. As it sputtered away, they saw dust coming from the mattress tied on top, as it appeared to be dancing in the sunlight. "What a drama," Ahmam thought to herself. They watched until the pickup disappeared down a hill. While still looking over the streetscape, Lihsiang said that when Chunlang moved in, Chen Tailan was one of the men sent by the moving company.

"So they only came to know each other about a half a year ago? I thought they must have been acquaintances since childhood."

"He works hard and as much as he can. Now he works as Chunlang's escort a lot with his pickup."

Lihsiang went on, "believe it or not, Chunlang did not find her first love until she was thirty-five. He was a motorcycle mechanic who worked near where she lived before.

You've seen her motorcycle, right? It's always in bad shape."

"So having her motorcycle repaired brought her a romance?"

"I really don't think it could be called a romance. It should rather be called a misfortune. Chunlang found this guy had a wife and children after they'd been lovers for some time. That's why she felt she had to move to another place."

"And moving brought her another relationship."

"Right. It's odd. Chunlang said she was a seamstress of children's clothes and never thought she'd want a relationship. She never expected everything would get overturned as she was about to enter middle age." Chunlang's story stirred up new thoughts in Ahmam's mind. "What is it like falling in love with someone for the first time in one's mid-thirties? First love is first love; it makes no difference when it happens," Ahmam thought. Her love for Linzhan sprouted at her nineteenth year and dragged on to her twenty-third year. It finally terminated in the second year of Linzhan's mandatory military service. Did it ever really blossom at all? The answer was yes. In their relationship, beauty was equal to danger. Linzhan did not know, or did not want to know, that Ahmam had waded across many bad waters by herself. Perhaps he even acknowledged it internally, but he had no way to help, so he decided it was Ahmam's love sickness. Ahmam had learned what it felt like to be betrayed in her early twenties, she insisted on hanging on, for she expected to see fruit after the blossoms. The fruit turned out to be bitter.

Ahmam got a student loan from a bank without her family's knowledge in her second year of college. She used the money for tuition to rent a place off campus and buy furniture instead. The building where she lived had been partitioned into seventeen units on each floor and rented to college students. Linzhan was the president of Ahmam's floor. Ahmam lived at the end of the hall, whenever she did laundry or used the bathroom; she had to walk past sixteen other rooms. Many of her roommates were from the department of physics. They organized a campaign to vote in a floor queen. Ahmam got elected. The responsibility of the floor queen was to treat all the floor mates to hot pots. The hot pot party was how Ahmam got better acquainted with Linzhan.

Linzhan published an article about the hot pot treat in their college journal. His writing on top of his good looks impressed Ahmam. She sent him a book, *Family Catastrophe* by Wang Wen-Hsin as a gift. Looking back now, Ahmam felt the book was a bad omen of their love. Usually it was the girlfriend who took the chance to break up while her boyfriend was serving in the military. But Linzhan dumped Ahmam while he was in full service. Ahmam would never give a book to her new boyfriends since "book" sounded the same as "to lose." Ahmam also regretted she had sent Juchi a pair of sneakers. He had worn them to run far away.

All these things mattered so much to Ahmam when they had happened, but now the devouring tides had withdrawn, leaving only ripples. "Do you know the difference between betrayed loyalty and loyal betrayal?" Lihsiang asked Ahmam, like they were thinking of the same thing.

"The former is like me and Linzhan, and the latter is like you and my brother."

"Is there a difference?"

"I believe so." Ahmam told her how she learned what betrayal was.

The place Ahmam lived her second year of college was called Back Mountain. The building lay under hills near several fields. Every day as she went in and out of the building, chirping birds accompanied her. She was content with her new lifestyle. Ahmam's room lay halfway in a hill; she could see earthen mounds when she pushed open her window. The first time Linzhan slept over was because he came to chat with her and they did not notice how late it was. Linzhan pretended to doze off as he held Ahmam in his arms. Not knowing how to respond, Ahmam pretended she had fallen asleep too. Near daybreak, Linzhan quietly got up to catch his first class. Ahmam, curling in bed, listened to the rustling as Linzhan put on his coat. She sat up right after hearing the door close. She touched her fingers to feel the warmth that Linzhan left on her hand. Linzhan left a note on the desk, telling her he'd gone for classes and asked if she cared to watch a movie together that night. Ahmam was excited; she inserted the note in her notebook. Later, when one of them stayed in the other one's room overnight, they'd carefully take their slippers inside so the floor mates would not suspect they were sleeping together. That was Linzhan's trick. Ahmam remember when she had moved in, one pair of his slippers were sometimes outside his door and sometimes not, but she never really dug into what it meant.

One day near the end of the semester, Ahmam told Linzhan she was staying with classmates in the dorm to study for final exams. Ahmam and her classmates progressed much faster than they had planned, so Ahmam decided to go home around midnight. On her way back during a moonlit night, she happily plotted where she and Linzhan could go for fun during the winter break. Arriving at Back Mountain, Ahmam walked directly to Linzhan's door and found his blue slippers were gone. A funny feeling came over her. She climbed up to the ground floor and walked to the side of Linzhan's window where she saw a dim light on inside. Ahmam shuddered. She approached the window to watch. Suddenly the lights went out. Ahmam heard a girl's soft voice and the rustling of clothes being taken off. Ahmam became angry. She ran back to Linzhan's door and knocked like crazy. She knew Linzhan would not answer because when they slept together, they always pretended not to be at home if someone knocked at the door. The senior from the physics department living next to Linzhan woke up upon hearing Ahmam's eager knocking, he was not irritated. Instead, he said understandingly, "Linzhan must be out now. No use knocking." Ahmam banged on the door even more furiously. Unable to ignore the knocking any longer, Linzhan finally got up. The girl with him was a senior, belonging to the same high school association as Linzhan. She leaped from the bed, opened the door unexpectedly and rushed out in tears. Ahmam was surprised by her sudden action, as she passed her like a wind gust with Linzhan's scent on her. It caused Ahmam to cry. She began sobbing, saying,

"I love you so much! How could you do this to me?"

"You love me? I don't feel it." Linzhan replied coldly.

He slammed the door in Ahmam's face. The slamming door made Ahmam feel as if a gun had shot her. The next day she couldn't write anything on her exam even though she had reviewed the subject with classmates earlier.

That was the winter break Ahmam had to sell couplet papers in the market. In her heart, she could not get over Linzhan's betrayal. Before the winter break, Ahmam left Back Mountain and its wonderful surroundings. She moved into an old house near the school's volleyball court. Every morning she awoke to the sound of volleyballs bouncing on the wall. When she missed Linzhan, she'd stand on the balcony and watch the volley-ball practice so the athletic profiles of the players could replace her thoughts about Linzhan. Linzhan had actually found the house; he took her to check it out because they had planned to live together. Linzhan's birthday was during the winter break, on January 25. He was an Aquarius, born during the sun's weakest time. Ahmam checked a horoscope book it said the lucky flowers for Aquarius were vio-lets and peonies, so she dug out some paintbrushes she hasn't used for a long time and completed two paintings of violets and peonies. Ahmam wanted to mail them to Linzhan before his birthday, so she walked a half hour to the post office and sent them by express service. Ahmam's mother nagged that painting was an activity reserved for rich people and if Ahmam wished to paint flowers, she should hope to be born in a wealthy family in her next life. Ahmam wasn't listening; her craving to get a reply from Linzhan made her absentminded. The day the mailman came happened to be the only day of good business for Ahmam's couplet papers. Ahmam thought it must be a good sign. At the end of her sales day, she packed hurriedly and ran out from the corridor of the market to read Linzhan's letter. Uncle Ahlu, who knew the Wu family quite well, teased her, saying, "this pretty little girl has a boyfriend now!" as his old motorcycle cack-led by. Ahmam put her index finger to her lips to hush Uncle Ahlu and smiled at him happily. The letter was still carefully preserved today, along with many other letters from Linzhan. Linzhan's handwriting was childlike, but his words were sophisticated. When the spring semester started, Ahmam arrived at her new place with many boxes. In despair, she collapsed on the stacked boxes. To her surprise, Linzhan turned up. He wore a pullover sweater and carried a bucket of paint. Without saying a word, he began painting the walls of the apartment for Ahmam.

Stunned, Ahmam remained silent. At last Linzhan spoke, he suggested they buy a rug at the flea market. As they walked downstairs together, Ahmam was told they would be riding on his motorcycle.

"You bought a motorcycle?" she asked.

"No, I just brought the one I owned from my hometown." he replied.

Ahmam imagined a scooter, but when she saw a Yamaha DT trail bike, she realized she did not know Linzhan as well as she had thought. During the fast ride, an obscure intimacy emerged between them. Holding Linzhan from the back, Ahmam wished she could get hold of her own life. Linzhan was humming a song Ahmam had never heard before the intermittent notes were sentimental. Ahmam was afraid she was going to cry uncontrollably, she forced herself to concentrate on Linzhan's foot while he changed gears. She was also afraid she wouldn't have a chance to ride with Linzhan ever again.

Despite her confusion about Linzhan, Ahmam rode with him for another three years. Ahmam's doubts about Linzhan's fidelity could never be remedied. The girl running out of his room, as well as the many other girls Ahmam imagined had fallen for him had overshadowed her trust in him. In the days Linzhan did not come over, Ahmam could not help herself from checking where his motorcycle was or she stood on her balcony, looking for him among the volleyball players. Once Linzhan really was on the court attending his physical education class, Ahmam called to him from the balcony, his fellow classmates did not let the chance of making fun of him go easily.

"What caused your break up, then?" Lihsiang asked.

"No clear reason. He just stopped taking me out and...after a while I realized he had broken up with me. My brother did not do this to you, did he?"

"No, he would not have done that." Lihsiang replied.

"You made it clear you were leaving him. You tried to make up for the gap between you and him. Even though it failed, at least you tried."

"I wasn't that fair though. I was selfish in some aspects. I think what happened between you and Linzhan was quite a different experience."

"A salty experience," Ahmam answered.

"Why salty?"

"Every day was soaked in tears."

Lihsiang nodded in agreement. Tomomi's singing suddenly went off-key; they figured she had tried to follow the music as she listened to it through her earphones. A moment of silence between Ahmam and Lihsiang was broken when Ahmam asked: "Lihsiang, did it ever happen between you and my brother?"

"Did what ever happen?" Ahmam pinched her, and Lihsiang said, "What? Extorting my confession?" But she shook her head solemnly. Ahmam was amazed. How could they never have had an intimate relationship during their long time as boyfriend and girlfriend?

"Did you do it? If you do, you should be careful," Lihsiang said knowingly.

Ahmam felt she had been hit by a quiet wave of thunder. A scenario as stupid as you see on TV where an unmarried girl gets pregnant was something that had indeed happened to Ahmam. She had been pregnant before. She walked around the circular market at the intersection, hesitantly. No one accompanied her to sign any papers. She forgot how she eventually entered the clinic; she only remembered she took off her jeans and put on the green robe for surgery. She was laid down at the surgery table oddly decorated with a dark snakeskin grain. A pale, expressionless nurse gave her a shot and then she gradually lost consciousness. She only vaguely felt someone using a thing with a handle moving up and down between her open legs, when the thing finally found its target, Ahmam went numb and passed out. Ahmam learned from the experience that a person regains his or her sense of hearing back first when coming back to consciousness. Before she could open her eyes, she heard another girl's voice crying, "It hurts, it hurts..." then her groaning was drowned out by the sounds of traffic outside the window. When she opened her eyes, she stared at the light beams filtering through the blinds; the florescent light tube above her head stung her eyes. She felt nauseated, which was the only sensation she could remember. Ahmam wanted to know how the doctor had performed the ritual of rewriting existence. She asked the nurse, but the nurse only scolded her for not taking proper contraceptive measures. Walking out of the clinic, the bright sunlight blinded her. She felt everything was melting into obscurity. The hue was exactly the same as the florescent light in the clinic. Since that time, Ahmam does not use florescent lights, especially florescent light tubes. The experience could be compared to a bleak morning in late winter, but all the blank spaces revealed by sunlight were filled with her agony. Her soul had gone astray. Looking at the soulless bodies passing by, she did not know which one was hers. Ahmam returned to school and ran into Linzhan. He knew nothing about what had happened. She felt their earlier encounters must have happened in her past life. As they neared graduation, some classmates saw Ahmam and thought, "Ahmam is no longer full as her name suggests. She is thin as a skeleton now." Ahmam wanted to grasp everything she desired, but the consequence was that now she had to use the same efforts to leave her love behind in the golden age of her life.

"Getting to know oneself by falling into a ditch first— what a bitter lesson about growing up." Ahmam sighed.

"You are saying Linzhan was a ditch?"

"Yes. His decadence was indeed attractive. Young girls jumped in and fought to try the stinky water in the ditch!"

"Like fishy things pursued by fishermen."

"What was my brother like?"

"He was like a cypress a thousand years old."

Ahmam burst into laughter. "How did a thousand-year-old cypress express his affection?" Ahmam asked. Lihsiang said there was no way to ignite a wet wood. "I see. You are Orange Jasmine, like your name. Though you and my brother are both plants, you like to be in cities but my brother belongs to the humid forest." "We'd be the perfect couple if I could resist material seduction. Life in the mountains bored me; he could get so excited when a tree grew an inch taller. I was only happy to receive the new clothes my mother mailed me, your brother never noticed if I looked or dressed differently. That's why I left."

"Hey, you have pimples. I never saw pimples on your face before." Ahmam said changing the subject.

"That's exactly the price of living in a city. The air in the forest was much better." Lihsiang recalled the old days with sentimentality.

"So has he ever done anything that touched you?"

"Of course he has. He named every tree seedling with my name, Lihsiang number one, Lihsiang number two…your brother said because of that, he could love me for his entire life even when I was away," Lihsiang said in a light tone.

Ahmam felt it was impossible to digest such an idea. She asked herself if she could love a person in this way. Why must her relationships be like that of teeth and a delicious meal? It would taste so fine at first but then the bits stuck between the teeth would become disgusting if left for too long. The delicious part never lasted. The delicious moments of her love usually happened in railway stations. Linzhan lived in eastern Taiwan. She lived in the west. Before they set out for their respective hometowns, they'd say good-bye to each other in the train station with a conversation like this:

"Did you eat watermelon today?"

"Yes, I did."

"Was the watermelon tasty?"

"Very tasty."

Then they'd cup their hands under their chins, pretending to eat watermelon eagerly. Onlookers were confused by their words and gestures, which was what they intended. It was a code shared only between the two of them. They were the watermelons and "eating," meant, "missing you." In translation, the conversation was:

"Did you miss me today?"

"Yes."

"How much?"

"Very much."

After such a secret and sweet farewell, they got onto the trains dreamily. But once the train began moving, Ahmam usually couldn't help but cry uncontrollably. The insecurity from the first betrayal had happened in such a short space in time and the second betrayal Ahmam conjectured conveniently happening during winter break since both Linzhan and the girl he betrayed her with went back to the same town. Thus, each winter break was cruel torture for Ahmam, a wound that never could be healed. Even now, going back home was a struggle. Ahmam thought of the pickup carrying the mattress. It was so real and solid; nothing was concealed. Unconsciously she hummed: "You are the needle, I am the thread. Needle and thread never go apart…" Ahmam thought she might marry any man who was willing to carry a mattress for her.

"Ren Chunlang will open a flower store when she comes back to Taipei after the New Year. Chen Tailan supported her very much; he decided to remodel the office of his moving business into a flower store for Chunlang. His pickup would only deliver his princess and flowers in the future," Lihsiang said. Ahmam wondered what kind of flowers Ren Chunlang was going to sell. Lilies, perhaps?

The whiteness and the prevailing fragrance would be a perfect match to Chunlang's invariably dark outfits. "Chunlang was born in the wrong time. If she were born later, she'd have become a fashion designer instead of being treated like a cheap seamstress." Lihsiang added. Seeing Ahmam not responding, Lihsiang teasingly asked,

"You're jealous, aren't you?"

"I suddenly think it's a good idea to marry a man like Tailan." Ahmam smoothed the bangs over her forehead, her mind tried to probe the simple and pure love of Chunlang and Tailan.

"Come on. You'd deny the possibility of any development with a man like Tailan at first sight."

Lihsiang had seen through Ahmam. Ahmam knew that if an unkempt man like Tailan turned up to carry a mattress for her and send her home with his truck, she'd begin to detest him. Wasn't Big Bear at the car repair business of Ahmam's building a good example? Ahmam seldom saw him standing straight; he was always lying under a car but never failed to stick out his head and wave his greasy hand to say hello wholeheartedly whenever Ahmam walked passed. In the beginning Ahmam was surprised every time, but later she became used to this carefree communication and would stop by every now and then to chat with Big Bear. Ahmam recalled that once Linzhan said she was especially attractive to blue collar people and should take the position as a manager in his family's factory. Ahmam did not take Linzhan's words as a compliment; she felt insulted. Nevertheless, after so many years, Ahmam realized Linzhan was indeed quite observant. The last time she moved, she got on the truck with two movers stripped to their waist after all her stuff was loaded. Sitting between them, Ahmam enjoyed listening to their singing. Then they found they forgot something so they decided to drive back to their business first. Ahmam vividly recalled that among the rough wooden partitions, the movers smelling heavily of cigarettes and alcohol were stunned to see her at first but immediately joked happily,

"You guys also move people?"

Another one squeezed a dollar bill into her hand, saying,

"For you to buy some candy."

Ahmam looked at the bill and realized it was a sheet of notepaper printed like a bill and she laughed with them. When they got on the truck again, one of the movers introduced himself as Wu Ming-Chieh, which sounded like "no virtue." Ahmam laughed wholeheartedly, and thought how her mother regretted being married to the Wu family. That time Tziyang even worried about her; she wondered if those movers had fooled Ahmam until she saw that Ahmam had so much fun with them. Ahmam understood that she could be so carefree with the movers only because she knew they would only be in each other's company for a short time, she knew she would not develop a relationship like Chunlang's.

Tomomi yelled to them inside, telling them in awkward Chinese that she had made coffee, so Ahmam and Lihsiang entered and closed the door. "You are from Tokyo?" Ahmam asked Tomomi.

"Yes, Tokyo."

"Tokyo is a very fancy city, right?"

"Fancy?"
"Beautiful city."

"Yes, it is white."

Tomomi struggled to find a Chinese word. Lihsiang corrected her that if she meant, "clean" she should use *Gan-Jin*. Tomomi seemed to understand some things but was still confused on other points. She stood up to play music. Ahmam noticed she was playing "Sukiyaki" and said, "Gosh, what an ancient song. It's unusual for an eighteen-year-old to like this song.

"It's unusual for an eighteen-year-old to fly over to Taipei alone, too." Lihsiang added: "So I gave her a Chinese name, Ping-Ping, like duckweed."

"Ping-Ping suits her well, floating on water, encountering anything randomly." Ahmam agreed.

"But Tomomi didn't like it. She wants us call her by her Japanese name." Lihsiang said.

Ahmam teasingly noted that in this apartment, three women from three different generations constituted quite an amazing combination. Ahmam figured Lihsiang was seeing someone. She inquired and Lihsiang admitted,

"I've been confined on the mountain with your brother for too long." Ahmam giggled.

"Don't laugh at me!"

Lihsiang told her during the cold days not long ago, Zou Lu stayed over one night. "Sleeping with a man does make a big difference. I always have very cold limbs; Zou Lu was like a heater. I felt so hot in the night I had to kick the blanket aside." As she said it, she laughed impudently in a way that Ahmam seldom saw in Lihsiang. My mother unexpectedly showed up the next morning, she thought I was out so she let herself in with the spare keys I had given her. I hid in the blanket, plotting how I should say hi to my mother when Zou Lu stretched his head out and said hello to my mother first." Lihsiang laughed wantonly when recalling the ridiculous manner of Zou Lu.

"So will you and Zou Lu go steady?"

Lihsiang shook her head and laughed again, saying, "I think I am in love with a young guy. I met him when Tomomi and I went to a pub together. I told him I am over thirty, and he said that I must drink lotion instead of putting lotion over my skin. You should hear him speak. He's so funny. Lihsiang laughed, but suddenly her attitude turned serious, almost reflective before explaining her analysis that the gap between she and Ahmam's brother was in their lifestyles, the one between she and Zou Lu was the difference in how they perceived things. Now Ahmam remembered she actually knew about Zou Lu earlier because of the time Lihsiang asked Ahmam to go to the hospital with her. Lihsiang had peritonitis because of an earlier abortion. They were told that the suction did not clear out things in her womb thoroughly, which caused the inflammation. Walking out of the hospital, Lihsiang wept it was the most humiliating moment of her life. Had she stayed in the forest with Ahmam's brother, nothing would have happened. It was a rainy day with lightning flashing in the gray sky; the anxious faces rushing in and out of the corridor were lit by the lightning every now and then. Tears were running down Lihsiang's cheeks. Observing Lihsiang who had left everything behind, Ahmam asked her if she felt especially attached or emotionally dependent on a man the next morning after she had slept with him.

"To tell you the truth...I no longer feel anything,"

Ahmam looked at Lihsiang, unbelieving, and asked, "So you have transcended to another level?"

"To tell you the truth, yes, I have reached another level."

Both of them laughed at Lihsiang's "to tell you the truth," Ahmam wondered how Lihsiang got there so fast. Before Ahmam could ask her question, the doorbell rang. It was Lihsiang's parents; they had come to take her and Tomomi back home to Yangming Mountain for New Years. Lihsiang's mother scowled all the time. Lihsiang's father, a doctor of Chinese medicine, smiled and gave New Year's wishes to everyone. A Filipino girl who worked as their housekeeper also came with them. She spoke to them with her accented English. She helped Lihsiang take her luggage downstairs. They gave Ahmam a ride to the railway station. Taipei at this time was like a woman taking off her makeup—all the big sales had been put away and all the stores were closed. The only lights still radiating were the warning lights around construction sites. It was still too early for Ahmam to take her train home; she and Lihsiang rubbed their hands in the cold and looked at the darkening sky.

"Sometimes I forget there is a sky in Taipei," Ahmam said

Lihsiang touched her head to express her understanding. Lihsiang asked Ahmam if she remembered visiting her home and playing mah-jongg on the second day of New Years two years ago.

"You lost but refused to pay the winners." Lihsiang laughed at Ahmam's childishness at the time, and added:

"Say hi to your brother for me. I do regret not becoming your sister-in-law."

This time Ahmam touched Lihsiang's head understandingly. Both of them insisted on watching the other leave first, but Lihsiang actually had to go first because there was no reason for her parents to wait with her. Before they departed, Lihsiang told Ahmam,

"You are such a delicate girl; you should be taken care of by someone. I hope you find him this year."

"I hope you and Tomomi find your 'satisfactory lan' this year, too."

"What is 'satisfactory lan'?" Tomomi asked.

"Lan is like Chen Tailan's lan, like a wolf if the character's radical is replaced by a dog."

"Wolf?"
Tomomi was totally confused why in the Chinese New Year people would want wolves; she figured it must be some kind of tradition. Ahmam and Lihsiang laughed, so Tomomi laughed with them, her canines showed when she laughed out loud.

"It's hard to believe she is only eighteen."

Lihsiang shook her head. Ahmam knew what Lihsiang meant. It was not Tomomi's being eighteen that was so unbelievable but that her own age of eighteen had grown so far away. Did they accept how old they were now? Ahmam had doubts.

"Say hi to your brother for me."

Lihsiang rolled down her car window and reminded Ahmam again as she waved good-bye. In the station, Ahmam bought a sandwich and a tea egg. When she was about to eat them, she saw a homeless old woman crouching by an iron gate. She thought the woman might need some help and approached her but as Ahmam moved near, she immediately took her cloth-wrapped baggage and moved in another direction. Ahmam realized she should not disturb other people's situations; the old woman might mistake her kindness as an attempt to expel her from the station. For both of them, the New Year holidays were a torment.

First Visit Home

Most of the people sitting on the fiberglass seats in the bus station next to the railway station had dozed off while waiting for their buses until they heard the two aged homeless men yelling at each other from deep in their chests with venomous anger. One of them wore a pair of pants with a big hole in the bottom, his bruised buttocks were revealed to the embarrassed spectators. The other man had both his legs amputated; the trouser legs were empty. They shouted at each other across the rows of seats, the spectators were so engrossed they did not want to leave until the loudspeaker and the impatient conductor's whistle urged them to get on the buses. Some travelers reluctantly stood up from the corners and walked toward their boarding gates, some glued their heads to the windows to see the later part of the show after they got on the bus. The bus moved falteringly into traffic. Ahmam thought again of Tailan's pick up and the mattress jolting along its way. She also thought, not really eagerly, that she had forgotten to ask Lihsiang her mother's response on finding her daughter sleeping with a man. What would happen if it had been her? Thinking of this, Ahmam unconsciously held her breath. She knew that had it happened to her, she'd certainly have been saved the trouble of this trip home now. She had last gone home only two or three months ago.

One of her cousins, Bouchi, was getting married. Ahmam's mother told her she must come home for the wedding because they were short in the number of unmarried mates for the ceremony. It had been a long weekend. Ahmam could not get a bus or train ticket, so her mother made arrangements. She told her to wait at a highway exit for one of her uncles to pick her up. It was a windy day; Ahmam sat on the highway ramp worrying about her safety. After a swirl of dust blew by, Ahmam heard someone ask "Are you Wu-Ahmam?"

She nodded but couldn't open her eyes right away. When the dust finally died down, Ahmam saw the truck in front of her was not the pickup described by her mother but a giant semi and the man standing in front of her was not her uncle. The man told her he was her uncle's co-worker; their employer switched their shifts unexpectedly, her uncle asked him to give her a ride. With great difficulty Ahmam climbed up into the container truck and admired the spectacular view. About nightfall, a voice from behind surprised Ahmam; she turned to look and saw behind their seats was a sleeper berth, with a man who had been taking a nap inside.

"Ahmam, are you tired? "

"Do you want to sleep for a while?" they asked her.

"No. She replied quickly, I can rest well just sitting here."

So the two drivers switched at a rest area. The new driver must have gotten a very good rest, because once he was behind the wheel, he sang all the way. He told Ahmam, "Being a truck driver is not only a tiring job. The worst part is that you don't get respect from people. A butcher just got a contract from the music business, and now they call him the butcher prince. I should become a singer, and you can be my background vocalist." Ahmam laughed but did not offer any response. They arrived at Ahmam's village by midnight; the truck was too big to drive into the small village, so the singer walked her home. As soon as she heard the container truck, Ahmam's mother grabbed her coat and rushed out to find her daughter. When she saw Ahmam she seemed relieved but still complained, "Why did you guys come so late?"

She insisted on making hot tea for the driver before he hit the road again, she gave him a big bag of chicken legs right before he left.

"Now you can be a chicken prince," Ahmam said to the singing driver

This confused her mother. The young man put down the teacup and thanked Ahmam's mother before leaving.

"What kind of game were you playing with that guy?" Ahmam's mother asked.

In the nick of time the lights had gone out, so she did not see Ahmam's bemused expression. The next morning Ahmam dressed herself in a long skirt and stockings, she put on some makeup while her mother continually nagged her, saying things like; "The bride is many years younger than you. I don't know why you want to be an old maid. I am so miserable. My children don't establish their own families, which will be very bad for my karma." Many of her younger cousins who were also bridesmaids called her from the porch. "Sister Ahmam, hurry up! We are driving to pick up the bride at Plum Mountain!"

Ahmam smiled; she was ready. As Ahmam was going out to join her cousins, her mother nagged that she had dressed so plainly that her cousins would out shine her. Ahmam's mother accompanied her daughter to the door. She smiled to the other bridesmaids cordially and said,

"Your cousin has lived in Taipei for too long. There are a lot of things here that she feels alienated from, so you girls must show her the ropes and help her out."

They laughed and knew they'd better not respond; they just glanced at Ahmam knowingly. Ahmam winked at them. Only the youngest cousin, Hsiaoyun, a first-year junior high school student, couldn't help but giggle. Her giggling suggested that her aunt's remark was off base, someone beside her nudged her arm to stop her. They knew their aunt's temper well.

"Do not hang around; you girls must return during auspicious hours," Ahmam's mother bade them in an authoritative tone.

Ahmam turned to follow her cousins passing through a bamboo fence, she heard her mother singing: "Looking back, our conjugation was out of our love, which resulted in the change of my body..." It was a very old song about a nurse falling in love with a married doctor and getting pregnant; she had to exile herself because of her shame.

"Out of love?" Ahmam was sure that her mother wasn't singing about her love with her father.

Their car soon left their village behind, and Ahmam fell into a reverie. The father of the groom was the director-general of the farmers' association, a position that brought him good connections, so every seat of the hundred-seat round table was occupied; there were still guests without places to eat. During the feast, Ahmam naturally became a topic among the relatives, for both her single status and her unemployment.

"She is useless," someone said.

Ahmam's mother wore a flowery dress that Ahmam's brother brought her from Southeast Asia. She began to pack up the unfinished dishes with several plastic bags and added:

"A university graduate is not as capable as these girl performers."

Electronic music accompanied a group of young dancers on the stage and the host was telling dirty jokes. By the end of last December, Ahmam's mother called and urged her to come back again, saying express mail had been sent there for her. Ahmam knew it was a trap, she told her mother

"Open it and you will know what it is about."

"How can I know your business by opening your letter? She snapped, I don't read. You come back and read it yourself."

Ahmam begged her cousin Hsiaoyun to check the letter for her. She was told the sender was Hsinhsin, a boy she knew from a party in her freshman year. After so many years, the only address Hsinhsin had known about Ahmam was her hometown address, so he sent her a Christmas card and a recent picture. In the card he wrote "Celebrate Being Single!"

Hsiaoyun read it and asked, "Why would you celebrate being single?" Ahmam did not explain; she told Hsiaoyun it wasn't important. She appreciated the unusual well wish. Ahmam was sure that if the letter had been from Linzhan, her mother wouldn't have had to beg her to come back; she would have gone anyway. Thinking of this, she sighed. The last letter she got from Linzhan, she did not actually get it from him. She saw it when she opened one of his drawers. On a purple paper with the letterhead of another department, Linzhan had written in big characters with a blue marker.

"I hate you as much as I hate this world."

Ahmam realized Linzhan wrote this to her because he knew she checked in his desk all the time. She felt she had been busted; she took the paper and folded it carefully. She did not ask Linzhan about it; she pretended it never happened. Perhaps that was why their hopeless relationship dragged on until Linzhan began his service in the military. Ahmam found the purple letter not that long ago when she was tidying up her things. Each stroke of Linzhan's writing was still alive, compared to the faded words Juchi had sent her through a fax. Ahmam was astonished when seeing the almost blank fax pages. Their love had faded into oblivion; no traceable evidence remained. "Blank papers are the proof that it was nothing but a dream. We never took pictures together, I've sold all the presents he gave me…" Thinking of this, Ahmam felt her past loves really had gone like ashes blown by the wind.

She heard the snores of her fellow travelers here and there. In the dark Ahmam has no idea where they were; surely they have arrived in the drier, warmer middle of Taiwan. After some time, the landscape gradually emerged in the first gleam of daylight. Even without looking, Ahmam could distinguish the contours of her unique village. Ahmam knew that in several minutes the night would be replaced by day. She inhaled the fragrant breeze emanating from the surrounding mountains and waters. The rhythms of nature had been progressing peacefully; as Ahmam's senses were awakened her hometown came into view. It seemed that Ahmam was the only spectator among the bus passengers of this dramatic succession of night and day. The sky cleared up, sunbeams filtered through the wild trees that formed a canopy over the road. The wheels of the bus sounded different as it drove past the red bridge. She observed that early risers had already started working on the riverbanks. The water's surface was like a thin layer of glass, for winter was a dry season. During this season, farmers are not able to pump river water to their fields; they had to carry buckets of water for their grain crops.

"My shoulder blades are deformed." Ahmam's mother often complained about the hardship of carrying water. But there could be something worse: she countered, floods. Floods were the worst nightmare. Everything was gone with the water; you cannot even save your own provisions. Sometimes the storms fell upon the villages like they had a particular mission to destroy things; the villagers had to take their livestock and evacuate. After the flooding was over, they came back to reestablish their homes from nothing. Ahmam witnessed a super typhoon when she was in elementary school. The floor of her home cracked and water spurted up like a fountain. She approached the spring with her head to let the water sprinkle over her face that infuriated her already-worried mother; she slapped Ahmam across the face. When the floodwaters receded, Ahmam found some coins, her mother told her she used to find drifting lumber, lost ducks and sometimes even rabbits and piglets. In those times snakes would ignore people and enjoy the sunshine by curling up on the rocks protruding from the riverbed. It was hard to believe the mild streams gurgling peacefully by the fields most of the time could become so ferocious. Even while away from her hometown, Ahmam could imagine what was happening at home in August and September. The farmers carried the water to their fields in the warm air. Watermelons were already round and full about to be harvested. Farmers smiled from ear to ear, exposing their stained teeth. Their smiles were their highest reverence to the gods for saving their harvest from inundation. They looked up to the sky from time to time during the harvest season and shouted, "No floods this time!"

When the summer was over, the streams dried up and became a part of the autumn landscape. Silver-grass thrived at the riverbed and waved when an autumn wind blew by. Ahmam thought it was even more fantastic if silver-grass bloomed, the villagers said, "If silver-grass blooms, we will have a flood next year." Relying on the mercy of nature, they were good at predicting the pulse of the earth.

The bus passed the bridge. Ahmam had been told before the bridge was constructed, people had to wade in the water to get to the other bank. "When my father was marrying again, his bride lifted her gown and walked over in the water because my father couldn't afford to hire a sedan chair for her." Ahmam's mother said. Not only was her step-mother from the other bank, her late mother was also from there. In the second day of the New Year, married women had to go back to their parents, but each trip across the river was a life-threatening thing for the obliged daughters from the opposite side. Thinking of this, Ahmam took a look at the awesome bridge.

"Water is like a dragon. It brings us good things but it also devours." Ahmam's great-uncle once said.

Ahmam's mother responded, "My Ahmam is a dragon princess; she is docile."

Ahmam believed she was arguing with him instead of praising her daughter. Ahmam walked up to the bus driver to tell him she was getting off. Her mind was still lingering on past memories. "Happy New Year!" The driver said to her, she saw there were dark circles under his eyes. Ahmam returned his New Year's wishes before getting off the bus. A gust of wind blew her long hair, blocking her sight, she heard someone calling her from the bus. "Young lady, you forgot your totoro!" She instinctively stretched her empty hands to check then rushed back to the bus door. At that moment the fat totoro was squeezed through the window, she caught it and took a good look at the person who had been sitting beside her the whole trip. It was as if she were seeing him for the first time. He had a seriously burnt face; the facial features were hardly recognizable but the tenderness on it was unmistakable. Ahmam smiled at him wholeheartedly, she immediately realized it was the first time she had really relaxed and smiled since she began preparing for the trip home. The bus moved on toward its next destination. The dust it raised disturbed the bright red flowers by the road. They stood in the cool air, emitting their sweet fragrance proudly. It was the morning of New Year's Eve.

New Year's Eve

Everything started earlier in a small town.
The streets were pleasant and the lives of people in the past were still imaginable. Several young men stood on a bamboo scaffolding to install a new marquee at the cinema. The facade of the ancient theater was modernized instantly. On the ground, the advertising panels for the movies to be played during the New Year holidays still smelled of oil paints. The thick, colorful paints reminded Ahmam of young girls with too much makeup. As she walked past the theater, the assemblage of panels was not complete yet, Ahmam couldn't tell all the movies that would be playing. One of the young men whistled at her. Ahmam ignored him.

There were three periods when she entered that theater. Memories of these visits surfaced one by one. It was more than ten years ago since her last visit. Ahmam felt she had aged as the theater had. Rumors about the demolition of the theater never stopped. Ahmam no longer felt close to it. Memories of the old building were like the loosened threads on a skirt's hem; no one cared about them until the loosened thread caused the skirt to tear. It is much more convenient to buy a new one than to fix the old one. Ahmam told herself. No one wanted to stir up troublesome memories.

The wooden stand selling calamari porridge in the narrow alley beside the theater was still there, a canopy of tarpaulin with blue and white stripes had been added to its top. Four characters sloppily carved over the red painted panel read: "*Generating Profit, Creating Prosperity.*" This stand has been here since Ahmam was allowed to go to town by herself. It was indeed profitable. There were always more customers than seats; many ate their porridge while standing and leaning against the wall. Their sweat often dripped into their bowls. The stand attracted more people than the theater. Back then; Ahmam's mother always asked her to buy the leftover soup from the porridge if she knew Ahmam was going there to watch a movie. She said, "They get rid of it when the calamari runs out anyway. It's a good deal."

Ahmam was embarrassed to make her request to the vendor, who seemed very nice, so she told her friends not to let her mother know when they were going to town. Strangely, as the business of the stand became better and better, the wife of the vendor got more and more round. Her belly was only flat for a short time between the long months of pregnancy. Most of the time she moved around clumsily. The flower patterns on the baggy maternity dress she had worn many times had faded. Once Ahmam saw a customer glance at her and the vendor while biting the crispy deep-fried calamari, saying, "thin as you are, you are quite capable of reproduction."

The vendor did not respond; he only laughed and kept stirring the porridge in the cauldron. The wife washed bowls one after another in silence; Ahmam never saw them speak to each other. Ahmam remembered when she was in her third year of junior high, she went to a movie with a classmate when they came out of the theater, it was raining. Ahmam and her classmate sheltered themselves under the blue canopy. Realizing their money could only buy one bowl of porridge. The vendor gave them one more, free, but Ahmam was too embarrassed to take it. Her classmate took it and said happily, "We got to buy one get one free today!"

"You really love movies, don't you?" The vendor asked Ahmam, with a touch of fondness in his voice. She was too surprised to answer. Ahmam forgot everything about the movie she had seen that day, the tender words of the vendor and the ghastly stare of his wife were forever etched in Ahmam's mind.

Ahmam could still recall the mismatched swollen torso and the appalling gaze of the woman.

She thought of the soaked calamari, whose pulpy eyes and pale cut-open body were the most inharmonious statement of death. Of course Ahmam had not thought so when she was younger. She was often hungry and envied her classmates with allowance who sometimes climbed over the wall and snuck off campus to buy food. They carried soup in thermoses, when the bottles were opened, the classroom would fill with the scent of dried bonito, stewed bamboo shoots, and coriander. Sometimes they were shared; those that did not get enough even licked the bottle lids. Ahmam never joined them; she sat in the corner and hoped her stomach would not rumble. When she was really starved, she naively wished that one day she could marry the calamari porridge vendor. When Ahmam enrolled in senior high school she was given some allowance, but the tasty porridge made by the vendor was no longer available. The gossip was that one night the vendor beat his wife and ran away. Ahmam never wanted to believe it; how could a man so tender beat his wife? She said she believed the real reason he left was because all the town's people joked that the vendor's good looks and his small alley business seemed like an odd fit, so he quit. Ahmam's cousin Chiuyin warned her, "You think a nice-looking man wouldn't beat his wife? Don't be fooled by the looks of men."

The youngest sisters of the seven girls the vendor had left with his wife, twins, were in junior high school now. Everyone said they were born unlucky; they wouldn't have a bright future, the only thing they could do was serve others as maids. Ahmam noticed the panel with the carved characters which read, *Generating Profit, Creating Prosperity*" were pinned upside down, she felt her mouth watering, the taste she desired long gone.

Ahmam turned from the alley and walked to the restroom of the railway station. She gave five dollars to the old woman selling tissue paper at the door of the restroom. Ahmam told her tissue paper was not necessary because she only needed the restroom to change. She took a long skirt from her luggage to show her. The old woman tried to return the money: "You don't have to pay to change," she insisted. "I should pay. I need to use your facilities." Ahmam replied refusing to take back her money.

The ability to change her clothing assured Ahmam because her mother was hard to please when it came to how she dressed. She put on white socks to go with her brown loafers and carefully adjusted her collar in front of the mirror. She also put on some lipstick before zipping up her baggage and getting ready to go home. After Ahmam had changed and walked out, the old woman praised her. "You are beautiful," she said. The old woman watched her intensely then asked, "Would you marry my son? He is a hardworking man; he would be good for you." Ahmam laughed, not knowing what to say to her.

Once she stepped out of the station, a group of taxi drivers jostled toward her, competing for her business. Ahmam did not know whom she should choose, so she told them she was walking home and turned into an alley to find a taxi there.

"You must be tired from the late-night ride. Coming home for New Years?" a taxi driver inquired. He gently guided her towards his cab.

"Yes to my mom's house." Ahmam replied absently.

The road had been widened during the past decade. Beefwood trees flanking the road moved backward as cars drove by.

"Are you married?" the taxi driver inquired.

Gosh, Ahmam uttered. The issue never stopped haunting her.

She wondered silently, do I look so old everyone assumes I must be married?

"No, not married," Ahmam said.

"Then why did you say you're going to your mom's home? An unmarried girl has one home only. Your Mom's home is your home, isn't it?" He looked at Ahmam from the rearview mirror with a serious expression. Ahmam smiled apologetically. She was going to see her mother anyway. The taxi approached her village and stopped at a spot that was the last stop because cars could not drive through. Ahmam took out a five-hundred-dollar bill and gave it to the driver. The driver hesitated taking it. Did she say something that offended him? Instead he asked: "Are you Redhead's daughter?"

"Redhead? Who?"

"Sorry, Redhead is Lin Jinju. We have called her Redhead since childhood. Is she your mother?" Ahmam nodded. Now she remembered the man, he used to sell honey in their village on a very noisy motorcycle. She recalled a late autumn afternoon when farming work was over and the weather had made everyone drowsy. The sound of the motorcycle woke up her mother; she got up from her bamboo bed and rushed through the doorway with her shoes barely on. Ahmam heard her mother yell,

"You have to make such noise, huh? You could wake the dead!"

Ahmam expected a quarrel to explode, and felt ashamed that her mother's shouting was equally annoying as the motorcycle.

Suddenly, laughter followed, when the motorcycle was gone, her mother brought back a bottle of honey. She explained,

"That was my childhood friend. He is from another village. We fought a lot then. Even now, we are both old and barely see each other, but we still fight when we meet."

The honey contained in the wine bottle was like treasure; each day Ahmam stealthily dipped into it with a chopstick and tasted a drop of its heavenly sweetness. One day the stool she used to stand on to reach the honey on the shelf slipped because of a loosened leg, Ahmam fell. The bottle dropped and broke into pieces. Honey dripped slowly on to the floor from where the bottle dropped to the stove. Ahmam ran out instinctively and hid by a ditch until nightfall. By the time her mother found the accident, ants and flies had already overrun the tasty honey. She had to light a fire and burn it.

"You goddamned girl! Do I owe you something from my past life so you waste my things like this?" she said with distain in her voice upon finding her in the ditch.

Ahmam groaned and insisted it was not her; even later when her mother coaxed her saying, "Tell me the truth. I won't punish you if you tell me the truth." That night Ahmam dreamed ants and flies were glued to her skin so she could not move. The next morning Ahmam wanted to escape from home for the first time in her life. She was thirteen years old.

"I will give you a free ride for the sake of Redhead!" the driver said, he squeezed the bill back into Ahmam's hand.

"No, it's hard work and you should be paid." Ahmam left the bill on the seat and closed the cab door.

"Give my New Year's wishes to your mom," he said out the window. Ahmam thanked him and watched him drive away.

I forgot to ask him why he quit selling honey, Ahmam thought. She held her totoro doll and walked on the path that was still slightly muddied by the morning dew. At the end of the path, several households gathered at a mild slope. The clouds thinned the sunlight. Among the thriving canola fields, an old banyan tree with interlocking roots acted as the border that had been growing there for at least a half-century. In the tranquil morning, the sound of ocean waves could be heard. An elderly cow cried sadly in a low voice. Ahmam wondered whether it would survive the New Year. Following the path, Ahmam saw her aunt's house. Above the indigo door, a stone slab with a relief of artistically inscribed characters, Loyalty *and Filial Piety*, were visible. The last time Ahmam was there was because of her uncle's funeral, the first time she visited was for her grandfather's funeral. The Wu family had divided very early. Partially because Ahmam's mother did not get along with her mother-in-law, this further separated Ahmam and her siblings from their grandparents.

Ahmam met her grandfather for the first time when she was five years old. He was on his death-bed with his eyes shut. Ahmam remembered it was a warm, sunny day; as she played on the hill around her home, she heard weeping from the foothills. She did not go to find out what had happened; she fell asleep. She awoke in a mosquito net, her ears ringing from the chanting of Buddhist scripture and the smoke of burning paper money choking her. She couldn't open her eyes.

"Ahmam must be caught by grandpa's spirit," she heard one of her relatives say.

"Damn".

"She is just a little girl, why take her away?"

"We never got a thing more from the Wu family than any others, why sacrifice my daughter?" her mother protested.

No one dared to respond. Ahmam was told later that at that moment, someone took a pamphlet of Chinese medicine carefully written in her grandpa's calligraphy, declaring that her grandpa had wished to pass on the book to Ahmam.

"What can this do for us? This impractical thing is not even edible," Ahmam's mother complained.

Ahmam took the pamphlet; her eyes became alert again when she saw the nude diagrams in it. The pamphlet did not really belong to me after all, Ahmam thought. It was eventually blown away by a typhoon.

The pigpen in their yard that had been built of adobe bricks had become too small for the pigs and was now mostly abandoned. A big yellow dog was tied up there. A red paper with the characters, *Domestic Animals Multiply,* was attached to the concrete column of the house. The dog was not idle. Seeing Ahmam, he barked furiously.

Ahmam knew another reason her mother did not interact with her uncle was because her parents were from the same village, and her mother was afraid everything she said or did would get back to them and cause her trouble. She often said, "Bad news can spread thousands of miles, not just in this small village."

According to tradition, married women paying the first visit to their parents after the wedding should not stay later than dinnertime. When the smoke of the kitchen chimney rose, they must depart and set out for their new homes. Ahmam's mother did not even stay till dinnertime; she took off not long after noontime with the chickens her stepmother had procured for her. The chickens were called "leading the way chickens." One must be male and the other female. They were put under the nuptial bed to predict whether the bride would give birth to a boy or girl first. Ahmam was told that her mother got up right after the rooster crowed at dawn to check on which one had walked out from under the bed first. Seeing the hen walk out first, the nineteen-year-old bride shed a tear. Ahmam's mother explained, "It meant I would have a baby girl first and my in-laws might be disappointed.

Fortunately the prophecy of the chickens was incorrect. Ahmam's mother gave birth to three boys before Ahmam. The mistake made by the chickens was less serious than the one made by the matchmaker. When Ahmam's mother was shown a picture of the first-born son of the Wu family, she said yes because she was eager to leave her own family. One day before her wedding, while she was cutting rice in the field, she spotted the man in the picture teasing some girls. The image of a good-looking man with styled, shiny hair gave her hope for a happy new life. It was not until her wedding day that she realized that the man in the picture was not her groom but his younger brother. She fell into a despair that deepened later when most of the fortune of the Wu family went to the first-born son.

Ahmam's memories about her cousins had gone blurry, she still recalled that her oldest cousin loved dog meat and was an expert on the topic. He could tell the age, sex, and whether a female dog had delivered a litter from the first bite of the meat. Ahmam avoided this cousin as much as she could, the big guy would capture her easily. He teased her by kissing her or pinching her cheeks. When Ahmam was in elementary school, this cousin was in senior high school, hanging out with gangsters. Ahmam took a sympathetic glance at the aged yellow dog again. It was fourteen years old now, limping and deaf, but his barking was still powerful. He had only survived to this day because the cousin was in jail. Looking at the yellow dog, Ahmam saw her past ten years as well.

Aunt Meijou

When Ahmam arrived home, the house was empty. The auspicious character on the red paper over the door was all too familiar. She put her heavy bag onto the round table in the dining room. The sound scared the sparrows pecking grain off the floor. The breakfast left on the table suggested it had been eaten recently; the stains of pickled cucumber and peanut shells were evidence, as well as the still-warm pot of porridge. The smell of pork gravy lingering in the air was not her mother's work. It was from a pack of instant noodles that reminded her, yet again, of moments from her childhood.

When she was a schoolgirl, Ahmam was often awaken by this delicious smell around midnight. In order to be in the wholesale agricultural product market at five o'clock every morning. Ahmam's parents had to get up at midnight. They usually took two packs of the instant noodles from a cardboard box and quickly cooked them before they set out. Ahmam's father would call her to share a small bowl of the noodles before they left; it was her reward for locking the door behind them in the early morning. Since she felt hungry all the time, the instant noodles were the best reward. Ahmam was confused about why the smell was still hanging around. Was her mother eating instant noodles today? Ahmam felt uneasy. As she walked past the dark corridor leading to the kitchen, she saw an overturned urn that her mother had used for making grape wine. Over a redbrick counter, next to the stove, there was a white-skinned goose and a black-boned chicken. They were laid out on rectangular aluminum cooking sheets, with their gizzards and testicles set to the side. Ahmam could easily imagine her mother's big hands working on them, her nails sinking in their chubby bodies to fix them so she could drain the blood and pull off the feathers. She'd cut open their bellies with a sharp knife and pick out the inedible fat. After that she'd wash their feet by carefully stretching their web toes.

The only sound came from the rice cake steaming on the stove. A lit fire was roaring. The red, sticky rice cake must have been breathing in the hot steam from the bamboo steamer. Ahmam knew her mother must have carried the iron bucket the long distance to the rice-processing factory to grind rice for the cake. Ahmam's mother always prepared everything for the New Year by herself. Even though she had aged much now, she still did not want to buy ready made products.

The sun gradually emerged from the window over the stove. Ahmam smiled, she squinted to check out the sausages hung on the bamboo sticks to dry. The daikon julienne lay on red bricks for preservation. Seeing the foods for New Years made Ahmam's mouth water. The wind brought in fresh air, blowing past the rustling bamboo leaves and through the window. Beyond the backyard was a rebuilt white brick wall belonging to the house of Aunt Meijou, Ahmam's third aunt.

Aunt Meijou's lieutenant colonel husband was deemed a most successful person. Ahmam's mother said he was the kind of man capable of growing feathers. Ahmam remembered Aunt Meijou's daily habit of trimming her eyebrows with a small mirror; there was a picture of a famous singer on the back of the mirror. After her eyebrows were done, Aunt Meijou would attach false eyelashes that Ahmam thought looked like hanging coconut leaves. She'd then put on a pair of crocodile leather shoes that Ahmam had believed were cracked. And last, she always put a silk scarf around her neck. Wearing a scarf had been a habit of Aunt Meijou' even before she was given a prosperous life by her husband because she had a black birthmark on her neck. Ahmam heard women of the village joke that her aunt must wear nothing but her scarf when she made love to her husband. "And her husband must be wearing a pair of polished black leather shoes in bed," one of them added. They burst into laughter so hearty that it sounded like the roof of the house was being bombed. Aunt Meijou spent a lot of time watching movies in town. She also learned to play mah-jongg. She had fun in town until night fell. When she finally headed for home, she dragged her sandals and swayed her beaded purse arrogantly, walking past the dim households that had begun to prepare dinner. Housewives who were busy calculating the expenditures of cooking oil and soy sauce, preaching to their kids or sweating over a pot would comment jealously, "Meijou was a salted fish; now she is different."

Although Aunty Meijou was very careful about her looks, she was also absentminded sometimes. One time she went to another village for a wedding. She was bewildered as to why everyone was staring at her. She complained to herself, these women are so backward that they do not appreciate my sense of fashion. It was not until Ahmam arrived that she realized what had happened. "Aunty, your eyelashes are missing!" Ahmam exclaimed at first glance of her aunt. Aunt Meijou took out her mirror to check her makeup and found she had indeed forgotten to attach her false eyelashes. The women around her now understood what was wrong, they sighed and said in unison,

"That's it!"

There was a bit of sympathy in their voices. Ahmam remembered another day when her aunt had probably had a hard time when she was out of the house, when she returned home, she was furious to hear her husband humming a tune of a Chinese opera.

She shouted at him, "What a stupid pig! You can't even speak a word of Taiwanese after living in Taiwan for so long!"

Her uncle was trimming plants in the yard. Upon hearing his wife's scorching words, his hands froze for a second before he responded, "I do speak Taiwanese—f__k the mother."

The joke was passed around and became a legend in the village. Ahmam recalled that as her aunt was telling the story, she laughed uncontrollably. The laughter at the oft-repeated joke made Ahmam feel a deranged sense of time and space.

The image of herself as a flower girl at Aunt Meijou's wedding resurfaced. Someone had put make-up on Ahmam and sent her to hold her aunt's wedding gown Standing by the bride, Ahmam was surprised to see a drop of blood on the pure white gown. The blood had soaked through the white glove on her aunt's hand as she held the plastic wedding bouquet of red roses. On seeing the blood her aunt panicked, the wedding turned into chaos. It made the upsetting marriage of a local girl and a mainlander into an even more peculiar event. The bloody glove came from a lousy manicure; it saved Aunt Meijou from doing work in the kitchen for many weeks after her wedding.

"Not doing a thing with your own hands? You are not qualified to be a village woman," Ahmam's mother nagged her half-sister, who was actually closer to her than her other siblings. Aunt Meijou never cooked even after her finger recovered. It took her quite a long time to get used to her husband's mainland accented-Chinese. Word by word and sound by sound. As their communication improved, they quarreled more often and more furiously.

Their lives were not always blessed. In the beginning of the spring two years ago, several weeks before ancestor worship day, Aunt Meijou's husband, his name was Shen, flew back to his hometown in China. Just like buzzard hawks fly southward to the wetlands around estuaries, they gathered to weep. Uncle Shen was hit by a serious stroke while on his visit, it was in remote northeast China. Aunt Meijou immediately flew over to see her husband and for the first time met his first wife. The pride of Ahmam's aunt disappeared when she saw her husband. She had worried that her husband would choose to go back to his first wife; instead he abandoned both of them by passing away.

It was Buddha's birthday, the season for ripening mulberries. Aunt Meijou regained her toughness after her husband's death and brought his ash jar back home. She also received his retirement pension from the military. That's where the money to remodel the white-walled house came from.

In a remote field, a small, black dot was moving. It was a train taking travelers back home. As Ahmam squinted her eyes to watch the dust raised by the train, her mother's voice was suddenly behind her. She was humming, "May we ask you, mister, while you are seeding in the field industriously, how can I reach Taipei, the thriving city people are talking about? I am helpless, a poor girl without any support..." Her mother's voice resonated perfectly within her body; had she lived in a city, she could have been a soprano, but in a poor farm village, she was no more than a peasant who sang with other women once in a while. To people in this place, singing was a luxurious reward for a difficult life. Ahmam turned to look for her mother, who was now standing at the gate, talking to her sister-in-law while peeling a sugar cane. The early morning sunlight cast two slender shadows of the two stout women.

"You picked it before it turned sweet," Aunt Meijou said after she tasted it and spat out the chewed fiber.

"The rain did not come at the right time this year," Ahmam's mother replied.

She entered the house and lifted the lid of a bamboo basket to take out a small spot. She scooped a bowl of soup and sipped it with slurping sounds.

"Hey, it's New Years and you are still eating instant noodles? You should change your habits. The difficult times are over," Aunt Meijou said.

"Ahmam's father and I ate instant noodles often, when I go to his grave, I feel I should make some instant noodles in memory of him and those hard days we spent together."

Hearing that, Ahmam said, "So it is," to herself. She also yearned to take a sip of the noodles.

"How much of a New Year bonus did Ahmam get this year?" Aunt Meijou suddenly asked Ahmam's mother. Ahmam was surprised.

"Who knows. I believe it is not much. She never earns enough to support herself. I don't know what she is thinking. She chooses to starve herself in the movie business. I just don't understand why she doesn't want to dress up and work in an air-conditioned office in the hot summer instead of running outdoors all day and having herself tanned like a dried coal." When she began complaining, her speech took on the tempo of a string of firecrackers.

"I thought making movies was a profitable business." Aunt Meijou injected.

"That's a lie. People in the movie business are the least honest people. All the time I worry that Ahmam is going to get pregnant before getting married. When she enrolled in the mass god-knows-what department, I had no idea what it would make her into. People told me it was a program that taught girls to wear makeup and sit in front of TV cameras to report the news. I expected that once Ahmam became a reporter, she'd let every-body know how destitute our village was, thanks to the incompetent government. Who knows why she chose to take the hard job." Her mother sighed deeply and spat out the sugar cane dregs.

"Ahmam is near thirty, am I right? Is she seeing anyone? Aunt Meijou asked in rapid succession. Getting married too old is bad for women. It gets harder and harder to have babies."

"She never listens to our advice. Her fate is bad when it comes to marriage, thus I must worry for her all her life. We've all said even a bad husband is like an inexhaustible stockroom one can rely on; she should just pick one. Anyone is better than no one." All the girls from this village who went to the city seemed to come back with glamorous makeup, outfits, and high heels, but Ahmam always looks so slovenly. If no one wants her, she might remain an old maid."

"Don't worry, the man who's indebted to her hasn't shown up yet."

"Indebted, how true." Mom laughed and continued, "Marriage is indeed about debt. Women like me are either widows or are fighting with their husbands every day. Not a single day is peaceful."

"It makes sense that people say marriage is like a harsh lesson in Taoist philosophy, because no matter how bad you have fought with your husband, in the night you still share the same bed with him." Aunt Meijou said.

"That's right. Without them, we would be bored." The two women then laughed out loud.

Ahmam glanced at her mother speaking eloquently in the winter sun; she was deeply affected and lost in her conversation. As Ahmam was in her reverie, her mother suddenly rushed toward the kitchen and cried out, I've steamed it for too long!" It was not until that moment that Ahmam noticed the vapor violently dancing in the dim kitchen; the steam pot was hissing. Her mother was surprised to see Ahmam. She was both happy and pissed off. When she lifted the jumping bamboo lid, the vapor died down. She checked the cake and asked, "Are we having a rising year?" Though it was to see if the cake had risen enough, it seemed more like she was asking Ahmam. "You surprised me sitting there," Ahmam's mother said. "You could have turned down the stove for me. You are no longer a little girl and should help me with some work. Don't be like your sister-in-laws. They eat rice everyday without knowing the price!" Mom was still like that; she always started her conversations with nagging. Then she softened and asked, "Have you taken breakfast?" She pressed the cake slightly to feel it and smiled satisfactorily. Cutting a tiny piece with a knife she passed it to Ahmam. Ahmam did not stretch her hand to take it and the steaming hot cake burned her mother's hand. By instinct she dropped it. Both mother and daughter looked at the cake on the floor, her mother bent to pick it and started eating the part that had not gotten dirty. She said lightly: "You must be tired from the bus ride. Go to get some sleep." Ahmam worried that her mother would blame her for dropping the cake.

Remembering Lost Loves

Lin Jinju, Ahmam's mother, always cared about the cost of everything, even trivial things. It brought back a memory of an incident from Ahmam's childhood that she remembered very clearly. The only outing Ahmam ever took when she was in elementary school was three months before her graduation. Parents were supposed to prepare snacks for their kids. Lin Jinju took her to the market to find some food for her trip. They spent a lot of time browsing in every food stall. Ahmam could feel her mother's hand calculating numbers even as it was holding hers. Finally she selected an imported apple. Its bottom was shaped like five bent fingers. When they returned home, she tossed it to Ahmam after washing it, Ahmam failed to catch it; it dropped to the floor and rolled several times. Greatly upset by Ahmam's absentmindedness, Lin

Jinju slapped her hard across the face, leaving an imprint just like the five fingers of the apple on Ahmam's little face. The next day, Ahmam did not eat the apple; it was too precious. She forgot how long she had treasured the apple, it was at least until the apple's skin wrinkled like an old man's and it had dried out. Ahmam ate it anyway. She was appalled to see a worm in the core that seemed to stare out at her. She threw away the apple core out of fear and immediately looked around, afraid her mother might see her odd behavior.

Ahmam got on her feet and walked back to her bedroom. The room had been abandoned a long time ago. Several years ago a super typhoon hit the house. The expanded structure was torn apart, the four walls entirely destroyed. All Ahmam's belongings were gone with that storm or at best, exposed to heavy rain. There would be a period of time in which Ahmam's love letters would be found in neighboring farmer's fields. One of Ahmam's cousins, helped villagers who suffered from the storm apply for a subsidy from the government. Ahmam's mother was happy to be given fifty thousand dollars. That was one of the few moments in her life that she did not criticize the government for being a bunch of bloodsuckers. Ahmam slept in the living room for many years after the storm. The wicker chair had been Chung Jien's, (her father) bed ever since Ahmam could remember. The chair had been like a part of her dad. He crashed in the chair at night as well as in daytime and if it was daytime, he often slept in his work clothes; sometimes coins dropped from his pockets when he turned over. Ahmam had learned to watch and wait for these moments. She would scurry in under the chair to grab the coins. After a while she would be able to afford a movie ticket in town; sometimes she would even buy a picture of the movie stars after watching a movie. Ahmam did not spend all the money. Before her second year of junior high, she slid most of the money in her bamboo bank. Chung Jien had slept in that chair for more than ten years and Ahmam's long bamboo bank was full with the coins collected during those years.

When Ahmam was in senior high school, the village became a restless casino. People of all ages gathered under the small light bulbs to play. Older people gambled for fun, younger people hoped to earn money to cover their tuition. Chung Jien played but felt ill at ease as he was playing because as Lin Jinju played she yelled frantically at him from another table. Ignored by her parents, Ahmam hung out with her friends along the railway, she considered whether she should run away from home with the savings in her bamboo bank. Ahmam did not run away, instead she gave the bamboo bank to Chung Jien to make up for his gambling losses. "It's your money anyway." She said as she handed him the bank. Chung Jien held it, bewildered.

The September Ahmam first went off to college; Lin Jinju squeezed a bag of overly ripe oranges and gave them to Ahmam, she said as she handed them to her. "Take these, I was told that in Taipei's restaurants, a cup of orange juice is more than one hundred dollars; that's hellishly expensive." She took them but as soon as Ahmam got on the train and sat down, she ate the oranges as fast as she could; she did not want to bring them to Taipei. She considered calling home the next day but decided it wasn't her style. She waited and called home a long time later, after all kinds of freshmen welcoming events were over. When she finally called Lin Jinju scolded her bitterly: "You are a full-fledged adult. You never need to return—just like your father. Don't be too confident as a college student. I still don't know where to find the money for your next semester." The preaching lasted at least half an hour. When Ahmam told her mother that she had run out of coins for the pay phone, her mother finally concluded, "Your dad stayed in the field hut all day; he doesn't want to come home now."

Ahmam realized that once she left home, her father quit sleeping in the wicker chair. Chung Jien had built a wooden hut on some barren land near the riverbed. The sound of hammering could be heard during the summer. It was Chung Jien fixing up the hut with more wooden panels in case a storm came. At nightfall, as the smoke of cooking rose here and there, barefoot Chung Jien smoked his cigarette and watched the remote sky gradually turning dark. One summer vacation when Ahmam came home, she paid a visit to her father's "villa." She touched the smoky wood panels with her fingers; neither father nor daughter said anything. One night, while Chung Jien squatted near his hut, smoking and drinking, his lone profile attracted the attention of several young thugs. They approached him, kicking over his wine bottle. They took his cigarette and stamped it out on the ground to threaten him. As they pulled him inside the hut, they demanded he give them money. In the dark, shabby room, they kicked over more wine bottles. It was then the thugs realized they had merely caught a drunkard. Chung Jien searched the hut for a while but all he could find was a big head of cabbage. The thugs were stunned.

"This guy is poorer than us!" They shouted as they ran into the night.

When Lin Jinju learned of the incident and recounted it to others, everyone laughed loudly. Some said Chung Jien was such a poor man. Had they searched his body, they'd have found some pawn shop tickets!" Others said, "Mr. Wu was lucky; those kids were stupid to bother him." Ahmam laughed with them but when she lowered her head, tears flowed immediately. The last thing Chung Jien took from the house to his hut was a small propane tank and a portable stove. Several years later, Ahmam realized with some surprise that what she was doing in her apartment was repeating her father's behavior. Lin Jinju had observed the same thing. She had already decided it was because of the genes Ahmam had inherited from her father.

There were only two differences between Ahmam and Chung Jien. The first was that Ahmam stole her older brother's electric heater instead of a stove from home. The second was that in contrast to her narrow place that had been built illegally, cheaply and was cold in the winter and sultry in summer, her father's hut was by the waterfront with a view of the moon reflecting on the river. Of course Chung Jien wasn't completely away from home. When Ahmam's secret plan for getting a loan from the bank in order to move out of the campus dorms was discovered; Lin Jinju was enraged and Chung Jien was at home. The chance that he was at home and accidentally caught in the storm of Lin Jinju's rage was as slim as getting struck by lightning, he was just that unlucky. "Go to hell! Don't come back here, either of you!" Ahmam's mother screamed. Lin Jinju accused him of conspiring with Ahmam.

"Did you even bother to ask her why she wanted you to get the residential registry certificate? And you are her warrantor? Do you know if she fails to pay off the money, it becomes your debt? "

"You are penniless because you have gambled away everything! How many things have you done in your lifetime that were not mistakes? You could even go wrong ordering vegetable seeds by not trying to get a better price!"

"When someone asked you to deliver some goods, you did not even find out what goods you were delivering, it turned out to be stolen stuff! "

"Had I not pleaded with people everywhere to save you, you would still be in jail without knowing when you would be released. You are intoxicated all day every day, completely oblivious to the world."

She continued her rant, "why you don't just drink urine? Thinking of these things makes my blood boil!" Father and daughter from the same bad seed, doing nothing but making trouble!"

Lin Jinju's endless criticism was like corrosive acid. It did not stop Chung Jien from drinking his favorite mixed beverage, rice wine laced with a vitamin B energy drink. When this occurred it meant he had won money from gambling, which only irritated Lin Jinju more. She stated that she'd rather get run over by a car than stay in such a hopeless house. Of course Lin Jinju never left the house; she stood in the murky corridor and scolded Ahmam and Chung Jien for two hours. To escape from her cage, Ahmam imagined herself as a camera. The lens was fixed on Lin Jinju's lips that seemed to never cease moving. When the movement finally stopped, the camera turned to Ahmam as blood dripped from one corner of her mouth. She had killed herself by biting off her own tongue and Chung Jien was nearly drowned in liquor. Lin Jinju was stunned, her jaws opened wildly then a sharp scream broke out as the sparrows in the trees flew away. Ahmam grinned at her not-so-artistic directing; she was deeply excited by the creative exit she was able to conjure with her mind. The next day she received a bank statement, on it were her name and her father's name, Wu Chung-Jien. In elementary school, all the test papers had to be checked and stamped by a parent; just like the bank notice, her name and her father's name were together. That trip home, Ahmam did not say a word. She left in silence, Chung Jien went back to his hut quietly too, to relax and smoke cigarettes by the reflection of the moon on the river. Both father and daughter had lost their ability to communicate. Ahmam deliberately took a slow train back to Taipei.

It was June, the song of early cicadas and the heavy panting of the old train accompanied Ahmam northward. When the train arrived at the Yangmei station, the rain began. Ahmam decided to get off and transfer to a train heading east. At the station, Ahmam jostled among a lot of rain-soaked travelers under the train schedule board, she was vexed. After deciding which train she would take, she found a pay phone and dialed Linzhan's home number. As the call went through, she heard, "Good Day, Meihou Enterprise, may I help you?" The voice was one Ahmam could never forget. Linzhan? I... can I stop by? After a good moment of silence, she finally heard: Sure, you are welcome to come. The words that followed Ahmam did not hear, perhaps she was overwhelmed by Linzhan's permission or because the sound of kids in the background disrupted their conversation. Ahmam felt her hands shaking as she said good-bye to Linzhan.

When she arrived in Hualien, Linzhan's hometown, the sky had turned orange. She called Linzhan again, this time the person who answered the phone was a young man whose voice was beginning to change. He asked, "Is this Miss Chang?" Ahmam shook her head instinctively, she knew it was Linzhan's little brother; she also knew who Miss Chang was. She told him she was Miss Wu, "Oh," he replied. It seemed she wasn't entirely a stranger to Linzhan's brother. He told Ahmam that his brother was not around, Ahmam believed him. After hanging up, she decided to stay at the railway station and wait for Linzhan. Ahmam had fallen asleep in a seat. She awoke to an old man begging for money to pay his cab fare. Ahmam told him she only had enough money for her own ticket back home. The forlorn man stared at her unconvinced. He shouted, "unsympathetic!" Ahmam ignored his comment; she was not in the mood to care what people thought about her. As she checked her purse to find coins for the pay phone, two ten-dollar coins dropped from her purse. The old man rushed to pick them up as they started to roll on the floor. Ahmam shook her head. She went to a pay phone and dialed Linzhan's number again. His little brother answered again saying Linzhan was still not back, he promised to pass on her message. As she hung up Ahmam felt like she was drifting, just like the old beggar. He appeared to be chewing some meat in a bun. He had it bought with Ahmam's money. The smell of his food attracted a stray dog. He lowered the bun to entice the dog, as the dog happily approached the bun, the man threw the bun into his own mouth and looked at the destitute dog triumphantly. Ahmam swallowed. She felt sick about her own situation. Ahmam tried calling again, this time she finally got Linzhan. Ahmam suspected that he was slightly drunk.

"Can I see you now?"

"...Maybe we shouldn't."

Ahmam panicked. "Why? You said I was welcome to come." In the moment during Linzhan's silence, Ahmam heard the pay phone taking her coins one by one.

"We haven't been separated long enough."

"Three years is not long enough? How long will be enough?"

There was silence again. Ahmam had almost run out of coins.

"I need to borrow some money." She said quickly.

Linzhan replied just as quickly. "No problem. How much do you need?"

Ahmam waited a moment and said, "eighty thousand dollars."

"I will wire it to you tomorrow."

"I will pay you back in installments."

"No hurry. Just...don't use it to invest in movies; you can't make a living in that business."

The pay phone started beeping to warn that there were only seconds left. Ahmam gave Linzhan her bank account information quickly and then the conversation was over. Her trip put to an end. It was not that late when she hung up the phone. She found of all the money she had left, she was now twenty dollars short for a ticket back home. Ahmam loitered in the station, debating whether she should call Linzhan again. The homeless man was about to fall asleep in a corner of the station floor. Seeing that she was still hanging around, he asked, "Did you run away from home?" Ahmam shook her head. "No, I do not have enough money for a ticket back home, she replied sadly. The old man loosened a bag he had tied at his waist and opened a series of knots. He gave her back the twenty dollars she had lost, she thought, "Don't be fooled again." Ahmam took the last train back to Taipei. On the ride back, she realized that Linzhan's initial welcoming words were out of courtesy while answering phone calls for his family business. She was so stupid not to know that. Miss Chang was Linzhan's classmate. Ahmam had met her many times and felt Chang had threatened her relationship with Linzhan. Ahmam once tore up a picture of Linzhan and Chang together; now she understood that what she had torn apart was her own relationship with Linzhan.

Lin Jinju did not speak to her until she showed her the bank statement that proved she had paid off her debt. She knew that her mother's two hours of scolding was out of disappointment and frustration. She worked in the fields before dawn ever day, picking vegetables with her own hands and taking them to the market to sell. She never failed to pay Ahmam's tuition and was very sad that Ahmam just wasted the money. Ahmam did not think what she had done was wrong; she knew if she never tried her best to save her love, she'd regret it till her death. The time with a lover was priceless and she would choose to do it all over again if she was given another chance.

Ahmam was taking a nap in Lin Jinju's bedroom; it was a narrow, murky place. The ridge of the structure was held up a by a big bamboo trunk, and on the white plastered wall was a plaque inscribed with "Two Hearts Knotted Together Forever." Ahmam was told this plaque was Lin Jinju's only dowry. Ahmam's parents did not even have any wedding photos. Lin Jinju's memories of it had faded away. Every time Ahmam asked what her wedding was like, she always said: "I remember nothing." It took me twenty minutes to walk from my old home to my new one. When I arrived, your grandma didn't even lift her head to look at me. She was sent in a sedan chair; I was not as lucky as she was. My mother-in-law was already a grandma at the age I am now. I still have nothing from my kids." Ahmam still remembered her mother's complaint from many years ago when all her brothers were still single. Ahmam leaned across her mother's cinnamon-colored bed; she remembered that she forgot to tell Lin Jinju she had met the honey vendor. Ahmam looked across the window facing north, the seventy-year-old windowsill was decorated with broken pieces of ceramic urns, now so dilapidated. Outside the window, tree branches weaved creating a complex scene at the far end of her perspective. Drifting in obscure thoughts, Ahmam felt a pair of senile hands holding her. They belonged to a sad soul that was in tears; they seemed to open the door of Ahmam's soul and enter her memories.

Remembering Wu Chung Jien

in Jinju was in tears. Whenever Lin Jinju wept, everyone in the family had to witness it. Chung Jien was the opposite. Ahmam was the only one who had ever seen her father cry. One time was because of Ahmam's illness, another time because of his own illness.

When Ahmam was eighteen, in her last year of high school, something happened. It was one morning, as a lark stopped at her window, knocking on the glass in the weak light of dawn. Ahmam woke up alone in the house. As her mind stirred her body was still asleep. Something was wrong. Ahmam was supposed to get up, fry the leftover rice with soy sauce, and put it in her aluminum lunch box for school. She was supposed to pump water into the water tub that had dried out the night before.

But that morning she awoke feeling strange. Lying in bed, she felt as if her body was split in two, with one half of it paralyzed. She couldn't even sit up. At first Ahmam was happy, now she did not have to go to school since it was the day of final examinations.

She had skipped school once, pretending she was sick, but her teacher did not buy it; she suggested that the only part of Ahmam's body that ached was her hair. Now she felt lucky she was really sick. She had spent all night reading a romance novel, forgetting to prepare for her exams entirely; all her textbooks were still in her school bag. About the time of the school morning assembly, the telephone rang. Ahmam couldn't get up to answer it. Her entire left side was unresponsive. The sun moved, casting sunlight directly on her face. Flies, that had just visited the public toilets stopped by, seeming only to irritate the immovable Ahmam on purpose with the terrible smell they carried. The old clock chimed. Ahmam knew it was noon. The small satisfaction of not having to go to school was replaced by a growing hunger. Ahmam realized that everyone had traveled for business or school and no one in the entire village knew she was bedridden. She became frightened. She remembered that the circus was supposed to come to her village. As she heard the circus trucks approaching, she noticed only one of her ears was working. She could hear the unique voices that belonged to the performers. The sound of their iron trunks opening and closing and the blaring of a trumpet during someone's practice made Ahmam depressed. "I did not want to go to school but I do want to miss the show!" She screamed out loud but was appalled to hear her own voice was slurred. "How come my voice sounds like that?" She wondered growing more alarmed. Ahmam was desperate; she couldn't speak now, singing with the opera that she loved so much was now of no importance. The opera had started, there were thundering drums and gongs as the lead actress entered the stage with heartbreaking weeping. Ahmam was annoyed. Darkness surrounded her. She couldn't see anything anymore.

The old clock struck eight in the evening and Ahmam hadn't eaten anything for a whole day. She heard her mother say, "The bad, bad girl never returns from school; she must be having fun somewhere. I am going to break her legs to teach her a lesson!" Ahmam heard the light bulb in the kitchen being switched on. The wok was hissing on the stove. She heard water flowing from the bathroom. Ahmam knew it was Chung Jien cooking and Lin Jinju showering. She lifted her right hand to sweep it against a doll on the nightstand, the sound of something falling concerned Chung Jien. He came to check on what had happened saw her lying in bed and said, "Ahmam, you are still sleeping! Your mom is going to punish you!" He switched on the light and saw Ahmam was in tears as she struggled to speak with her deformed mouth. "Can't get up," she managed. Chung Jien rushed out to find Ahmam's mother. Lin Jinju usually wore an undergarment with double rows of buttons when she came out from the steaming wooden shower even on hot days, but today she had no time to put it on. She held it in her hand, cursing. "That goddamned kid!" She condemned her, declaring that it was Ahmam's karma because she always read books in bed without doing any work around the house. Though her mother cursed Ahmam, she nonetheless set herself to rescuing her child by quickly borrowing a pickup from the circus outside. Lin Jinju carried Ahmam on her back as they passed the vendors of barbequed calamari and fried spicy snails. The audience turned their eyes from the stage to the mother and daughter for a second. As she was being put in the pickup, Ahmam heard one of the actresses sing a sorrowful song in a high-pitched voice. Ahmam yearned for preserved guava and charcoal barbequed corn. In the summer breeze, She suddenly felt cold. Her mother tore down the theater's red velvet cloth embroidered with golden characters to cover Ahmam's body. She pinched Ahmam's left leg, asking, "Does that hurt?" Ahmam shook her head. The yellow tassels were on her face, swinging against it as she rode along. At the county hospital, Ahmam felt sensation in her body as an unknown liquid was injected into her. The fast-flowing liquid suddenly magnified the muscles, bones, and sinews. When it flowed to her head, she felt it was trapped, like water stuck in a pipe about to explode. At certain moments, it was like the lid of a steam pot, jumping as the air was evaporating. "How do you feel? We are scared to death, why don't you say something?" Lin Jinju pleaded. Seeing Ahmam's eyes closed, her mother worried.

"Be quiet, she is resting," Chung Jien said sternly in a low voice, Lin Jinju was awed by his demeanor. She thought this man now behaved like a husband instead of the loser she scolded all the time.

"It could be that something hit her head and blood has pooled in it," a doctor told them.

"What did the doc say?" Lin Jinju asked as she followed Chung Jien. He was pushing Ahmam's bed away from the exam room. "She hit her head, and the blood can't go through," he explained. At that time, all three of Ahmam's brothers were going to schools in Taipei, so Ahmam could only be taken care of by her parents in shifts. No conclusive results had been reached from Ahmam's examination. She had to stay in the hospital, observing all kinds of people coming and going.

It was the lunar calendar's seventh day of July, Valentine's Day. Heavy rain came with thunder, which was believed to be the tears from the constellation of the Weaver Goddess. When the rain stopped, Ahmam saw Chung Jien walking toward her from the direction where a rainbow shone. He held a red bamboo basket and there was something else red in his other hand. As he neared, Ahmam saw it was a bouquet of cockscomb flowers. As soon as Chung Jien entered the ward, he worshipped the Weaver Goddess quietly. The

Weaver Goddess was said to also be the protector of children. He told Ahmam, "Your mom is worshipping the goddess at home and at the family shrine. She made noodles, rice dumplings, and sausages for the worship and for you too."

The hospital organized a party for the holiday. Ahmam asked her father to push her to the lobby and leave her alone. At the party, Ahmam used a handle to turn her wheelchair and look around. With a lower perspective, she had a very peculiar experience watching just people's legs moving around. Some women hit the floor in high heels. Ahmam could feel the pompous air as they danced, and their hemlines swept over Ahmam's face. In the sweltering summer, Ahmam was the only one left behind in gloom. The low mood was like a puddle of water on muddy ground. As the rain continued dropping, the water had nowhere to go. It could only sink lower and lower. That night, her eye level was as low as that of a little child. The doctors who were in pale robes during the daytime were now transformed into elegant dancers. Ahmam was amused. But as her teenage melancholy came back, she opened the door with great effort and wheeled herself away from the party. It was the first party Ahmam ever attended in her life, and no one really noticed her existence. Ahmam suspected her resentment of parties when she was in college was because of this unhappy experience.

On the same night, when Ahmam was in half-sleep, she heard the doctor ask, "Who is

Wu Chun-Mam's Family?" Ahmam watched as her father smiled at the doctor and stood up. He stopped chewing the betel nuts in his mouth. "Come over to have a talk," the doctor said to him. The steps of Chung Jien's bare feet were like a slow, sorrowful song. Ahmam opened her eyes, looking upward to the sky and the shadows of coconut trees over the wall.

A thin fog blurred the moon, the voice of a vendor of rice dumplings was heard along with the hissing of a rice bran teapot accompanied his lonely voice. Chung Jien stepped back into the room and Ahmam closed her eyes to pretend to sleep. When either parent was around, Ahmam always felt uneasy. Her dad was in tears. He held Ahmam's hand and touched her tenderly. Ahmam was surprised. It was the most intimate moment she shared with her father in her life.

Not long after that night, the hospital found that something had contaminated Ahmam's X-ray negative during development, misleading the doctors to believe that she had a tumor in her head. The doctors still could not find the real cause of Ahmam's disability. Fortunately, despite all the confusion, Ahmam gradually recovered. She began to feel her left side and eventually could move it. After the excitement of her daughter's recovery, Lin Jinju felt angry about the hospital's erroneous diagnosis. She claimed she was going to sue the hospital, but her neighbors dissuaded her; they thought it was wiser to maintain a peaceful relationship with the hospital.

When all the lotus flowers wilted, lotus seedpods grew and their roots were ready to be picked. On that day a recovered Ahmam was on her way to meet her older brother who was returning home. She walked along a small stream and stopped every now and then to enjoy the landscape she had been unable to see for weeks. In the shade of a tree, Ahmam watched her parents wade in the lotus pond, their feet deeply buried in the soft mud. In the light of the setting sun, Ahmam thought their profiles were like unfinished sculptures of Michelangelo. She suddenly felt awed by the magnificent association. Taking a break in the field, Lin Jinju called to Chung Jien to take some tea. Ahmam realized why her voice was always so loud. Spending long days for so many years in the fields, one must shout to communicate with others.

That's probably why even her sneezing and farting were loud—Ahmam reckoned that Mom wanted to warn Dad that she was around all the time, and any noise she made was equal to saying "Don't be lazy!" Lin Jinju complained about Ahmam's timid personality. She said it comes from a bad seed. She regretted that the genes for courage were not in Ahmam. Lin Jinju was most pissed by Ahmam's nickname "mouse," which was what her male classmates called her. She said, "Raising a mouse...it will bite the rice bag and you lose all the rice." She did not want to raise anything that could cause her loss.

Filtered sunlight kissed Ahmam's face as she stooped over to check the typhoon grass. The number of marks on the typhoon grass would match the number of typhoons coming in the summer. There weren't any mark on them, suggesting that no typhoons were coming. That summer, unexpected thunderstorms dropped in quite often.

Lin Jinju would say; one clap of thunder breaks nine typhoons. In other words, a summer in which there was frequent thunder was a summer in which there would be few typhoons. That day the clouds flew fast. They did not slow down until the mountain peaks stopped them. Ahmam fell asleep under a tree. When she woke up, she saw her brother standing over her with a white lily in his hand.

He asked her whether she still remembered how they used to walk in the ditches between the fields to the mountain. They walked and walked until night fell, but they never got any closer to the mountain. "Isn't it stepping farther away as we walk closer?" she asked. He mimicked how Ahmam asked questions when they were little kids. Ahmam picked a vine from the ground and played with it by making knots and then loosening them; she laughed and said to her brother that she remembered nothing about it. In return, she told him another story about he would steal the bicycle cart from their mother to ride to town. He was nervous and paddled it hard to ride away without paying attention to his little accomplice who hadn't gotten on the cart. The bicycle dragged her and her knee was badly skinned. The scar still left a light mark on her kneecap. He had touched her head tenderly and asked, "Why didn't you make any sound?" Ahmam was too quiet during her childhood.

Her story reminded him that he would often give her a ride to the only bookstore in town and that while he was reading books in the store, he ordered Ahmam to watch the bicycle outside. "What a caring brother you are!" Ahmam laughed. Then her brother pointed to the small stream in front of them and asked if she remembered ever being dropped into it. Ahmam brushed her hair aside to look at the water carefully. She thought if she had fallen into a stream like that she would most likely be dead. At that moment a cicada made a hissing sound before rushing directly to the water. It had committed suicide, its body drifted away. Ahmam wondered if it was only her imagination, she felt the other cicadas on the trees lament for a moment and then begin to sing again in unison. "Is there any difference between one more or one less cicada existing? Ahmam asked herself. Would there be any difference in this world without me? She began to weep; her brother thought it must have been because of the fear of being killed coming back to Ahmam. He eagerly began to comfort her.

He said, "It was when the stream was dried; it was so dry the stream bed had cracked!" Her brother recalled how he tried to pull Ahmam up but couldn't, so he shouted: "Baby sister fell! Baby fell!" Everyone in the field forgot the stream had no water, so they immediately dropped their hoes and rushed over to help. Lin Jinju was the first one to arrive. As soon as she pulled Ahmam up, she gave her a hard slap on her face. Ahmam started to cry and began to breathe normally. When Lin Jinju looked for Ahmam's brother, he was already gone. Had he been found; there is no question Lin Jinju's punishment would have come swiftly upon him. Now Ahmam remembered. She remembered she cried louder and louder until her mother realized she had shit in her pants. Lin Jinju called Chung Jien to take Ahmam for a wash, but he was spraying insecticides, he had walked further and further away.

"I can't rely on you guys to do anything good. I must have owed you something in my previous life so you guys treat me so cruelly!" Ahmam's mother dragged her toward the water pump, and Ahmam took a glance at her father every now and then, hoping he would turn back to help her. After so many years, Ahmam was finally able to patch the fragmentary memories together of what she saw. Chung Jien was standing among the hazy spray, carrying the iron tank of insecticide on his back. Holding the tube, he moved slowly in the fields, like a turtle waiting for nightfall so he could travel to other places. Ahmam remembered the iron tank reflecting the sunlight. She had to squint to see him. The sun reddened her small face, as her mother washed her body with cold water. She could feel her mom's hand rubbing her skin.

The second time Ahmam entered the county hospital was because of her father's illness. It was ten years after her mysterious affliction. It happened one day, when Lin Jinju went to his shack to ask him about helping her seed the fields, this time he did not respond because he could not. His belly had swollen abnormally over his skeleton-like body, not unlike refugees starved to the edge of death. His hand still clutched a wine bottle and his face was distorted by pain. Lin Jinju called neighbors to help. Chung Jien was sent to the hospital. As soon as Chung Jien was admitted to the hospital, Lin Jinju went to a temple to ask the goddess about his fate. First she lite three incense sticks and told the goddess who she was and what she wanted to ask. Then she threw lots. The thrown lots were one front side and one backside three times in row, which meant the goddess was willing to answer her question. She had to wait till the right hour. The goddess was from China; villagers called her the Fourth Matzu. Lin Jinju was waiting for the divine medium to be possessed by the spirit of the goddess. The two divine mediums were the sons of the temple deacon. Lin Jinju sat on a bench, waiting and dozing off in the smoke of burning incense. She was awaken by the possession of the divine mediums.

She hurried to the altar and watched in awe as the two divine mediums tightly grabbed the sedan chair said to be carrying Matzu. The two strong men seemed to have difficulty in controlling the moving chair. Lin Jinju was amazed. The superintendent of the temple sprayed a handful of sand evenly on the desk, the two divine mediums began to hit the desk with a chair—no, they were writing something over the sand with the feet of the chair. Lin Jinju raised her question and the chair wrote the answer of the spirit, interpreted by the superintendent.

As soon as the superintendent said the spirit's last words "It won't matter; don't worry," the spirit left its surrogates. The two men collapsed. Lin Jinju was delighted. She hurried back to the hospital and happily said to her husband with her big voice, "Matzu said you will be okay!" Before nightfall, she secretly burned the spell paper given to her at the temple. Lin Jinju's attitude toward her father's situation was strange to Ahmam. She had rarely seen her mother act like that before. Nonetheless Lin Jinju did not forget to complain about Ahmam's not being helpful enough. Since Ahmam was jobless, at least she could run some errands. Ahmam was sent to ask people staying in other wards about possible cures being passed around among the folk people. The next day Ahmam brought back a wind chime. Lin Jinju was pissed: "I sent you to find a prescription and you spent money on this useless thing!" Ahmam explained that she was told wind chimes could fend off evil things that caused diseases. She knew a wind chime could make the lifeless sick ward less breathless.

"Go again to ask people. Maybe there is a secret prescription from ancient times but kept only in the family." The next day, Ahmam brought back several green leaves; they looked similar to aloe.

"Isn't this aloe? This is a beauty product not a prescription," Lin Jinju said. Ahmam threw them at the bedside table and angrily explained that they were for the treatment of liver cancer, not aloe.

"Don't give me that face, I am just trying to understand," Lin Jinju said. She picked up the leaves and rinsed them carefully. "Make juice with a blender and drink it with the shredded fiber." Ahmam said repeating what she was told. Lin Jinju made a big cup of juice with the leaves and fed it to Chung Jien. Then they waited for him to excrete poisonous things from his body.

It was the first time Ahmam's father had been hospitalized. She noticed, seeing the wild sparrows leap briskly outside the window made her dad show a second of frustration. Ahmam knew her dad, who had been carefree all his life, would not be able to escape his cage this time.

Ahmam walked out of the hospital and the happiness of being able to walk came back. She had "lost her footing" at eighteen years of age and in the following ten years living in Taipei, she had really lost her footing without even being aware of it. Being back in that hospital, Ahmam felt she was so old yet the air in the hospital still made her hair stand on end.

Ahmam took the night shift taking care of her father, so Mom could buy and sell food in the market the next morning. Without Chung Jien to drive her, she had to spend five hundred dollars to hire a driver each day. "It's very expensive. Can you give me a discount?" Lin Jinju tried to bargain with the driver.

"It's not expensive. It's round trip and I cover the expenditure of gas, not to mention I will carry the food for you." He looked at Ahmam, adding, "Your daughter is grown-up. Doesn't she drive? She's use-less. Hearing this comment, Ahmam admitted to herself that she was really useless. Not one of her friends knew she was from a poor family, she didn't cook and couldn't ride a bicycle; they figured her family must have helpers to do odd jobs for them. Ahmam never learned to ride a bicycle because her brothers carried her and when she was in col-lege, Linzhan gave her rides all the time on his motorcycle.

This night was the third time Ahmam was alone with her father. The second time was when Ahmam was the patient and the first time was when Ahmam had just entered junior high. It had been during the turning of summer to autumn, the school's dress code for girls changed from skirts to pants. Ahmam's blue pants were from elementary school; they were too short for her now. Her mother wasn't at home, so she had to ask her father to take her to town for new pants. Chung Jien swallowed a sip of wine slowly and got ready.

Ahmam knew he was going to take her to town. Under the moonlight sky, father and daugh-ter walked in silence, daughter behind the father. Following her dad's scent, a mixture of grass, fertil-izer, and cigarette smoke. Ahmam felt secure. This same profile was the "useless man, eating without producing" condemned by his wife. Chung Jien's response to Lin Jinju's condemnation was always "Fuck you, woman!" or to throw his wine bottle. Except for his cursing, he was a wordless parent. Ahmam had to think hard to remind herself that he still existed. He was like a left over dish, cold and easily forgotten.

It had been ten years since the last time they were alone together. Ahmam felt ill at ease on such an occasion. The words she wanted to say to him were stuck in the depths of her mind. Most of the time her dad was in a lethargic sleep. Once he opened his eyes and glanced at Ahmam with yellow eyes, she knew he was thirsty. On the sixth night his condition worsened. It was like bombs in his body were exploding one by one, blood flew everywhere. He was no longer able to sit up. A nurse handed Ahmam several narrow plastic bags, Ahmam looked at them, confused. "Tie one to your father's genitals so he doesn't have to get up to pee." The nurse demonstrated with her thumb.

Ahmam took off her dad's light green pants slowly. Tears flooded down. Ahmam wished day-break would come early so her mother would come.

It was probably the first time she wished her mother were around. She was afraid to pretend to be close to her sick parent. The strangeness between them throughout their life times made the intimate care unusually embarrassing. Ahmam's love for her father was obscure. That night when Ahmam timidly held her father's genital organ and fastened it to the plastic bag with a red rubber band, her father suddenly woke up. He pulled his oxygen mask away and shouted, "Don't bother! Let me die!" Ahmam was not surprised by her father's outburst; she was more shocked by his vanishing flesh and soul.

In the morning, after the market hours were over, Lin Jinju arrived. She wore a bamboo hat and held a bag of rice noodle soup in one hand. Upon entering the ward, she knew something was wrong. She put down the things in her hands and walked toward her husband. She lifted the sheet to check on him. Seeing Ahmam's work, She gave Ahmam a glance, thanking her for taking on such a tough job. Chung Jien was delighted to see her, the first words he said to her were, "you should change your temper."

"Mind your own health, my temper is my business." She fired back. She took the ointment to spread on Chung Jien's cracking hands. She turned to Ahmam and said, "Go home and get some sleep." Before that day, Ahmam usually left for home as soon as her mother arrived, but today she wanted to stay longer. Later in the day Ahmam's brothers and their wives also visited. Seeing many people in his room, Chung Jien asked anxiously, "Where's Ahmam? Is she gone?"

Lin Jinju rolled her eyes in the direction of Ahmam, saying, "Isn't she by your feet?" Chung Jien lowered his eyes. After making sure Ahmam was around, he fell asleep. Suddenly, he started screaming out numbers in a voice that did not sound like his own, then he said, "All my followers…"

Lin Jinju immediately bade them all to kneel down she said, "Your father is possessed by Matzu!" Chung Jien continued, "Wish everyone here good

health and blessings for everything you are doing!"
Having been quiet all his life, such elegant words
seemed to be his last wish as well as a conclusion
of his life. A few moments later he was at peace, as
if nothing had happened.

Lin Jinju felt the omen. She insisted on taking
Chung Jien home. That night he was at home again.
He wanted to be laid in his worn-out wicker chair.
Within two days of his return home, He stopped
breathing. The wicker chair was haunted by the
slight smell of Chinese medicine, the last memory
for the noses of the survivors. Later the chair was
burned to raise money for Chung Jien in another
world. In the crackling flames, the chair was finally
out of Ahmam's life.

She still wondered if the one wishing everyone health in his last days was really her father. As
Chung Jien lay resting in his coffin, Lin Jinju noted
that he didn't seem like her husband. Of course
Lin Jinju's wonderment was refuted as ridiculous.
Before his death, He said he wanted to have a sea
burial, explaining, "I always wanted to sail out to
the ocean when I was young." Ahmam was surprised that her dad, a farmer with his feet in the soil
all his life had an unfulfilled dream of sailing. Lin Jinju
did not want to bury him at sea; she thought it did
not make sense for a farmer to have sea burial. So
Ahmam stole a pair of his shoes and brought them
to the windy ocean. She threw them as far as she
could; the shoes were like two canoes drifting over
the wavy ocean. Though the water was furious, the
two canoes sailed ahead without sinking.

Ahmam found a letter in an iron cookie box from Chung Jien's friend. It said:

It has been a long time since our last meeting, but I think of you often. I've been working in the mountains for half a month. Yesterday I received two thousand dollars through the mail from my wife. I enclose the money with this letter for you. If you don't have use for this money, please purchase some rice next time it is ready for harvest. Of course you can keep it for later use if not for the rice. Please do not worry about money.

The friendship of old times has gone as people passed away one by one.

More New Year Memories

The atmosphere of New Years couldn't wash away the smell of traditional cough medicine powder with strong peppermint in it. Ahmam's longing for home in the remote country before her arrival was immediately erased.

The only thing new in this room was the portable closet made of plastic cloth, painted with rows of lovely small trees and small houses. In the closet were Ahmam's clothes that had survived the typhoon. She zipped it open to fiddle with her old clothes. They were like twenty-year-old stories shortened and extracted. In the bottom of the closet, Ahmam found a red school bag. It was also made of cloth, which was very fashionable during the days of canvas school bags. Ahmam never could resist the temptation of such a colorful and sensational object. Ahmam was given this red bag when she was starting the fourth grade. One night she heard the old clock tick several times during her sleep, a mosquito flew through the hole of the torn mosquito net, circling around Ahmam's ear. She felt a gust of wind; the mosquito net was lifted at a corner and her mom stroked her face tenderly. Lin Jinju was unusually tender that night. She licked her own finger and soothed the mosquito bite on Ahmam's face with her saliva and promised her daughter she would get her a new mosquito net. Chung Jien was asleep in a corner of the bed, snoring. If he turned a little bit he'd fall under the high feet of the wardrobe.

"This man is ugly even in sleep. But he is quieter when awake than in sleep." Mom sighed. She took off her dress and went to bed. Ahmam did not have her own room until she went to junior high school. Before that she slept beside her mother. Sharing a bed with her parents, Ahmam dared not make any noise at night. She'd grab some clothes to cover her mouth when she had to cough or sneeze.

Ahmam woke up the next morning and saw the brand new school bag. She was excited. She felt it was impossible to sleep again. She wished the day would break sooner so she could go to school with her new bag. Until the night Ahmam got her new school bag, her mother's late returns had been lasting for a while. Every night when her Chung Jien and Ahmam occupied the bed, both maintained as much distance as possible from one another.

Between the father and daughter was an inexplicable imbalance due to the absence of Lin Jinju.

Ahmam was mature for her age; she felt the oddity of a man and a girl sharing a bed even if they were father and daughter. Without her mother between them, Ahmam slept uneasily. With Lin Jinju beside her, Ahmam did not feel very relaxed either.

It was during this time, Lin Jinju had a new friend from the mainland. Ahmam knew because once she had taken a trip to the hot springs in Kuantzi Summit. It was not until Ahmam was many years older did she realize that the rare opportunity to take such a luxurious trip was because Lin Jinju needed her company to cover up something. She must have owed something to the mainlander, Ahmam rationalized many years later. Ahmam recalled that during their trip, they got in and out of cars many times and in a sharp turn around Tongopu, she was cast out of her seat but being so exhausted, she lay on the floor on her chest and continued sleeping. She thought her mother's hands felt funny, but it was actually the big hands of the mainlander carrying her back to her seat.

When she woke up, she was sitting between her mom and the man. A refreshing smell hung in her nose, one that was never found when she was with her dad.

During a transfer between cars, the man bought a pack of chips for Ahmam, she was too shy to accept it, so she hid behind Lin Jinju's floral skirt. Lin Jinju teased that Ahmam was pretending. She said, "Pretending to have little mind on the food." It was a Taiwanese proverb that the Mainlander did not understand.

He pinched the bag of chips, embarrassed. "She is not like you," he said. Lin Jinju did not understand why he said that, so she laughed to apologize for the impoliteness of her daughter. She explained, the little girl was inexperienced at traveling and seeing different things. She turned her waist and dragged Ahmam to her front. She forced open Ahmam's bending fingers to squeeze the bag of chips into her hands while encouraging her in mandarin to say thanks, thanks..." That was the best Mandarin Lin Jinju was able to pronounce. But when Ahmam managed to move her lips, she burst loudly into tears.

"Bad girl, you don't behave yourself when I take you out," Lin Jinju scolded. Ahmam felt wronged by her conclusion because in fact, she wanted the dark yellow bag of chips, not the green ones purchased by the man. Ahmam knew the flavors of the chips packaged in different colors because classmates who had allowance for snacks would share them with her. The dark yellow one was salty with the flavors of stew meat, but the green one was buttery and sweet. Ahmam never liked sweet snacks.

Ahmam was used to the noisy sound of men and women fighting all the time in her village; she was ill at ease during the trip with the silence between her mother and this man. She bit her nails all the way to the Kuntz Summit, a tourist attraction standing among many mountain peaks. They walked up the winding path and arrived at a small hotel whose facades had been yellowed by the sulfur in the air. Outside the hotel, Ahmam saw a caged, smelly black bear with a V-shape visible on its chest when it stood up. She felt its stretching claw would catch her. The fear of being caught by the bear made the loathsome excrement in the cage less of a concern.

In the hotel, Lin Jinju bade her to watch TV in the reception room where a stuffed, mounted reindeer was displayed on the wall above the TV. The show on the TV was about a stepmother torturing a young sister and brother by making them eat bug-bitten vegetables. In her mind, Ahmam screamed, "Run! Run away!" It was more like telling herself to run away than advising the two miserable kids on the TV. After a long while, Lin Jinju showed up from another side of the room, followed by the man. She was radiating steaming heat. Ahmam could smell the fragrance of soap on her. She handed Ahmam some clothes and urged her to follow them to the hotel room and take a bath too. Ahmam saw the man more clearly after the steam around her mom had evaporated. He had a big face, big ears, and gray hair. At his waist he wore a big yellow towel, with the name of the hotel printed on it. Ahmam stumbled toward the bath in their room but realized the door to the bedroom was suggestively shut, isolating her from her mother and the man.

After some moments the door was open again, and a strong fragrance overwhelmed Ahmam. Lin Jinju walked toward Ahmam. The hot air of the bath rested on the stone built pond, then blew past Ahmam in a gust. Ahmam tried to look at her reflection on the water, but the steam clouded her eyes. It reminded her of a story passing around her village: A mother addicted to mah-jongg took her little daughter to a hotel for mah-jongg one day, and after hours of playing, she remembered her daughter had never returned from the bathroom. She got up to check on her and found that the little girl had been drowned in the tub for hours. Ahmam was told the mother's addiction to mah-jongg worsened after her daughter's death. Upon hearing this story, Ahmam and her classmates ran whenever they saw a hotel, they imagined that hotels were places haunted by the little girl's spirit.

As Ahmam's mind was still engaged by these thoughts, her mother began to take off her clothes for her. "What are you thinking about? Hurry up. Never tell your dad what you have seen today, understand?" Lin Jinju turned her body and lifted her onto her lap, face up. She rinsed Ahmam's hair, she could feel her mother's strong legs as she lay on them, water washing over her head and long hair. Lin Jinju rubbed her scalp as Ahmam stared at a gecko on the ceiling. She continued to rub her body as white foam was produced from the brown sugar soap. That day Lin Jinju must have wanted to act like an ordinary mother because she was intent on bathing her daughter. She carefully cleaned up Ahmam's ears and greasy neck that looked like it was entwined by small black snakes, then her armpits and belly button. When her hand touched Ahmam's private part, she shrank a bit. Mother admired Ahmam's tiny body, "they say you were made by materials shared from both parents; do you believe that? You are so small, I hope when you grow up you won't be as small as your dad. He is small like three pieces of stacked tofu."

Talking about her dad, Ahmam wondered if he cared that his wife and daughter had been gone for a whole day. Probably not, unless he found his wine bottles were empty and he needed Ahmam to buy more for him. Their whereabouts and activities were never topics of discussion. At that moment, Lin Jinju poured water over Ahmam's head and the foam was washed away. Ahmam cried without reason. Lin Jinju thought it was because the water was too hot, she put her hand in the water to feel it and said: "the temperature is perfect. Why are you crying? Since I have had eyes, I've never seen a kid so hard to raise as you." She soaked Ahmam in the hot bath, this scared her the most, but not knowing Ahmam's fears, she inquired if Ahmam liked it or not. Ahmam felt the way she was being bathe was very similar to how her mother cleaned dead chickens or ducks. Her skin had turned white because of Lin Jinju's forceful rubbing. She pulled Ahmam out of the water. She dried her with a yellow towel and put her into a new dress. She said the dress was from the department store in Taipei.

When they walked out of the hotel together, the soapy smell of the three probably disturbed the black bear. Ahmam tightly grabbed her mother's skirt hem to catch up to the pace of the adults as quickly as she could. Lin Jinju laughed all the way and the man spoke in a foreign accent at intervals.

On the advertising boards all over the small alleys, were many animals that Ahmam did not know were painted, the coal barbequed food was familiar. A vendor was frying something in his wok and wiping his sweat with the towel he wore around his neck. As they walked past, he peddled his dishes to attract their interest. The towel reminded Ahmam of her father.

Mom often chided Dad for being a "trash ghost" because he used the same towel for one year by that time, she said, "you can even press grease out from it" All of the family would hang their towels at the same bamboo stick but keep their towels away from his no one would mistake which one belonged to him.

They had walked through the small town once, Lin Jinju's skirt had been wrinkled by Ahmam's grabbing, she hadn't decided where to dine. Ahmam suddenly had a crazy idea, she walked toward the man with a towel around his neck.

Lin Jinju stared at Ahmam first, then followed to see what she was doing. Seeing people coming, the vendor used the towel he had wiped his sweat on to dust the table for them. Lin Jinju was hesitant. She asked if the dishes here were expensive, the Mainlander smiled. He shook his head and ordered a lot of food for them. While they were still eating, Ahmam mimicked the way her mother always behaved at feasts: "Let's pack some food to bring home." Mom pinched her small leg several times under the table. That night they spent a long time dining, her mother taking several sips of the

Shao-Hsin Wine that was brought to Taiwan from China. The alcohol excited her, she began singing. The Mainlander tapped the table to make tempo for her.

Ahmam must have fallen asleep during the dinner; when she woke up it was morning, and outside the window the blossoming, white tungtree flowers decorated the green woods. The water of the hot spring was babbling. Ahmam rubbed her eyes. She did not know she had been carried to the hotel on the backs of the two adults in turns; she only vaguely sensed that beside the familiar smell of her mom's outfit, there was another scent. Lin Jinju and the Mainlander returned; She put the wet yellow towel aside and urged Ahmam to put on her clothes; they were going home. On the ride back, Ahmam laid her head over her mother's lap, sleeping. Lin Jinju was quiet, she kept her head low most of the time. When a sunbeam fell across the bench on which they sat, She unexpectedly yelled, "Damn!" She slapped Ahmam to wake her up and checked her long hair. She demanded, "Where did you play that you got head lice! Why didn't I see this yesterday? This little girl is like a ghost; her troubles could shorten my life so easily!" The Mainlander did not understand Lin Jinju. He thought he had done something wrong.

The days at home after their trip were difficult for both mother and daughter. The night they returned to their village the sky was reddened by the setting sun. Lin Jinju cut Ahmam's long hair in a booth at the foothill. Whenever she caught a lice egg she'd show it to Ahmam and sigh incredulously. The next day Ahmam went to school and felt indescribably uncomfortable without her long hair. Each night before dinner, their job was to catch her head lice. This was the only time in her life Ahmam was close to her mom; the odor from her armpits became one of Ahmam's most deeply rooted memories. What Ahmam did not know was that the unusual patience Mom showed during that time was because she was waiting for further word from the Mainlander. As for Ahmam, her eagerness to grow her hair back and time in front of a mirror to check if it was so eventually replaced her memories about the trip.

About a year later, on the first day of summer, Ahmam was helping take down the bed sheets hung outdoors to dry, the mainlander emerged from nowhere. Ahmam ran away immediately. She took a detour and hid herself in her aunt's house. She did not go home with the bed sheets until she saw the mainlander walk away. When she saw the sheets were dirty, Mom condemned her furiously. Ahmam did not resent the man at all, and at her age now she could relate to the unsettled feelings he must have experienced at that time. What would have happened if Ahmam had taken the mainlander to her instead of running away? She learned that the man had brought troops from Mainland China to Taiwan and stationed his camps around the river near their village. Perhaps it was fate. One day the Mainlander and Ahmam's mother encountered each other while Mom was washing her feet in the river. The lieutenant colonel happened to lift his head, and they exchanged their glances. Now Ahmam wished the "Old Taro" whom Mom sometimes called for fun would show up, but when Ahmam was little he already had gray hair, so he must have died even before Dad's death.

Lying in Mom's bed and recalling the trip with Mom and this man, unusual feelings surged into Ahmam's mind. If it wasn't for Dad's death, her memories about this man wouldn't have been summoned back.

Mom's bedroom was cramped, but it looked bright because all the blankets and clothes were well organized. The walls and the bed were structured from old, rough bamboo sticks. Bamboo blossomed once in a hundred years, so they were often cut for use before they had a chance to flower in their lifetime. Ahmam comforted herself by thinking, "They do not die; they just live in another way." This thought made her feel better because Dad also could be living somewhere in some way.

The poster on the wall was familiar, an old picture of a movie star, but in the poster the star's eyes were captured mischievously. On the top of the poster there was a slogan: "The activation of the cinema industry in Free China, the first self-made masterpiece, color widescreen movie." This poster had been here for years, but Ahmam had never bothered to scrutinize it until today. She read the slogan and wondered what progress the industry had made since it had been activated decades ago. She had problems finding a job to devote her passion to this industry. Her mother's words in her conversation with Ahmam's grandaunt were quite right; she wouldn't be able to work in the male-dominated world except as something like an assistant, organizing the costumes of the actresses.

On the bed stand was a bamboo bank inscribed with the words "Being a Fool Sometimes." There were some bills in it that Dad touched before his death, Mom gave the bamboo bank to Ahmam and told her, "This money is the legacy your Dad left you; don't spend it since it is the blessing of your Dad. When you are building up your own business, if you mix this money with your capital, then you will have a prosperous business." Ahmam never spent that money, not because she was obeying her mother's instruction, but because there was only two thousand dollars. If it were a lot of money, Ahmam probably wouldn't have resisted the temptation of spending it when she was in need.

Ahmam thought to herself: "It is life; who knows what will happen. If this doesn't happen, that happens. One can't choose what will happen." Ahmam wished the money wrapped in red papers would multiply, but only her foolishness multiplied. The money was given to Dad when he won the Mark Six Lottery. There were about ten red papers, suggesting that Dad had won ten times. But ten times in four years was not much. Dad wasn't a lucky gambler, and she had no idea how much Dad had lost during those four years. She only knew that the number of people who came to their home to collect money were much more than the number of people attending Dad's funeral.

During the mourning period, the survivors had to fold paper ingots for the deceased. They were told to recite the name of Buddha as one paper ingot was made, but Ahmam prayed the paper ingot would become real money each time. On the wooden shelf, Mother left many pieces of papers with different colors. Each one had a number, written in Mom's unskilled handwriting. They were the numbers Dad had screamed out before he passed away. Mom insisted, "Your Dad knew we wouldn't be able to pay back his debt, so he gave us these numbers to win lotteries." No doubt Mom continued to bet on those numbers, but she never won, and Ahmam wondered how much longer Mom would continue.

The daylight began to shine, and as Ahmam walked to the window, her heart spreading out in the sunlight.

New Year's Day

"Why didn't Dad want to sleep here?" Ahmam fell asleep again, disoriented from her thoughts. They exhausted her. When she woke up, she jumped from the bed to chase her oldest brother's seven-year-old son, Little Whale, who stood at the head of the bed, giggling with his new teeth showing.

Little Whale had bitten his aunt's face while she was asleep, so Ahmam grabbed her slipper, acting as if she was going to hit the little boy. He slipped away agilely, and when Ahmam chased him to the door, the four-year-old Bebe joined the chase, followed by the five-year-old twins of her second brother, Lili and Sansan, who also came to tackle their aunt in a pile. Ahmam was immobilized by the squirming bodies of her nieces and nephews.

Why had all the kids turned up at the same time? Ahmam gathered that all her brothers and their wives had returned. Scowling at Little Whale, Ahmam considered what action she should take next. Mom was busy in the kitchen. She was delighted to have all her children and grandchildren around. She smiled, her false silver teeth glistering. Ahmam caught Little Whale by surprise and gently smacked his face as revenge, not expecting the boy to begin crying like a collapsed water dam. His mother took a sharp glance toward them, and Ahmam's heart throbbed a bit.

Ahmam hated to be injured on her face; she had a scar that was evidence of some crime to her face in her childhood. "When you were little, I couldn't take care of you because I had to work in the fields, so I tied you to a bench, and your bandit like cousin Ahbiao sneaked over and bit your little face. You cried so loud, like the most heartbreaking thing had happened..." Mom said she ran toward her daughter from the other side of the hill, and the perpetrator had already escaped, laughing crazily under the midday sun. This story made Ahmam feel embarrassed whenever she met Ahbiao, who was five years her senior. He really acted like a mountain bandit.

"No, that scar on your face is actually from your Mom's bicycle accident. She did not park the bike appropriately so you fell off, and your face hit a sharp rock on the ground," Ahmam's third aunt said.

Her uncle's wife refuted her sister-in-law. "No, no, no. Actually, it's from a fight between your parents.

One time your Mom was outrageously pissed off and she broke a wine bottle, and a glass shard ricocheted off the ground and scratched your face." Ahmam felt this version made more sense because few of the rice wine bottles at her home were taken back to liquor store for the refund. Most of them were broken during the fights between Mom and Dad.

The mark had faded with time; it was only noticeable if one scrutinized Ahmam's face closely. Ahmam still cared about it, possibly because she didn't know its cause.

Everyone gathered in the living room as an appliance store delivered a twenty-inch TV. The storeowner was chatting to Ahmam's oldest brother as his staff was setting up the antenna. The kids were playing with the remote.

Ahmam felt odd; this was a scene played out in the city, not a farming village.

Ahmam's sister-in-law handed her a pair of high heels, saying, "My feet grow bigger each time I have a baby. I used to wear a size sixty-six, but now I can only fit into sixty-eight." Ahmam tried the shoes on and they were perfect. She took them happily but wondered when she'd ever wear high heels. Mom looked at Ahmam accepting the shoes indifferently and invited Ahmam to go the hair salon with her right then.

As mother and daughter left through the living room, the conversation between Ahmam's sisters-in-law could be overheard, along with the noises of someone frying something in the kitchen. "You are not happy to go with me?" Mom asked. She patted Ahmam's shoulder, saying, "Tomorrow is the first day of the New Year; don't wear your sister-in-law's old shoes."

"What's wrong with wearing her shoes? I don't have newer shoes anyway."

"You are so easily bought off. It's just a pair of old shoes. You don't make enough money for new shoes? And, you are still not seeing anyone at all, are you?" Ahmam shook her head and kicked rocks on the road, saying: "I was told my thick eyebrows and high cheeks are bad for marriage, and that my husband might be killed, so I'd better not get married."

"Bullshit. You have soft hair. A girl with soft hair is destined to be taken good care of by a good husband." Suddenly her mom approached her and looked into Ahmam's face closely. "Good, no wrinkles. No one will marry you if you have wrinkles." Being so close to her mom's eyes, Ahmam discovered that her mom's eyebrows were tattooed on so she did not have to paint them on when doing her makeup. The rigid inky eyebrows seemed separated from her facial skin, glancing at them made Ahmam feel funny. Her mom looked like a Southeast Asian woman with darker skin and darker eyes than was normal for a Chinese woman. She knew if she told her mom what she thought, she would be sad. Ahmam remembered once when she came home that her mom's dark skin had turned darker, but she did not inquire as to why. Mom just said in a sentimental tone, "Those young Thai and Indonesian workers all call me Mom." Ahmam realized that her mom took odd jobs during the fallow season. Mom found a peculiar comfort from hanging out with the immigrant laborers.

They walked passed some grand single houses standing in the middle of the fields. They were built when the economy was good. Some bachelor mainlanders married young girls from Southeast Asia when Taiwan was thriving, and many stories both happy and sad followed the cross-cultural marriages.

Mom felt confused by Ahmam's expression, which seemed to be neither particularly happy nor really depressed. They turned into a narrow alley and saw a rotating barber pole with black and white stripes and a childish handmade sign that read "Kueitzi Hair Studio." Yellow towels were hung over the handrail. On the colorful plywood door, a mirror reflected the profiles of Mom and Ahmam in the dim light. Ahmam noticed that when Mom was walking, her left leg still limped slightly. It was caused by a fungal skin infection that their doctor called snake tinea. Ahmam's older brother told of how her mom often cried out in pain late at night, claiming the snakes were invading her body and causing intolerable pain. She said the pain was just as bad as the pain she experienced when giving birth to Ahmam.

Ahmam, whose zodiac sign happened to be snake, had no words for her mom's comment. It seemed she was blaming Ahmam for inflicting the pain of delivery a second time, but how had she managed to attack her mom from inside her body this second time? At the time of her mother's attacks, Ahmam had hardly thought about her mom at all. How could she have played any role in it? The doctor told Mom that the cause of snake tinea was because she was under great stress. It was hard to imagine Mom could be under "great stress." To Ahmam, she was like pampas grass spreading wild across the land. It was tough, and people who tried to pluck the blades might be cut by their sharp edges.

They pushed open the glass door, and the buzzing hair dryers warmed the whole place. A voice inside yelled, "Welcome!"

Mom said to Kueitzi loudly, "This is my daughter. Remember her?"

Kueitzi smiled. "How could I forget?" She looked at Ahmam and asked absentmindedly, "Do you have a boyfriend?"

Mom replied, "No. If you know anyone suitable, introduce him to us. We'll let the young people go out and see if it works."

Kueitzi was taking out the hair rollers for a client, saying, "You are matchmaker yourself, aren't you? You don't have any candidates?"

"She never listens to me; my connections are all shit to her. Girls will become ill-tempered old ladies if they don't get married. But my words are no better than gusts of wind to my daughter." Mom made some sounds as the apprentice was massaging her neck and shoulders. The powerful hands must have made Mom feel good.

"You remember when you sent Ahmam here to learn how to do hair? Luckily she did not stay, or she would be like me, standing all day long, washing one head after another. In this village, I've washed so many heads. Their black hair turned to gray, gray turned to white, and eventually they went to another world...I've seen so many things."

"You know, providing these children with an education costs a lot of money...thinking of it now, I do not know how I survived those days," Ahmam's mother said.

A boy was washing Ahmam's head, his hands were lathering with shampoo. Ahmam recalled that when she graduated from elementary school, Mom had sent her here to learn some skills, but Ahmam was sent back home after washing several heads.

Kueitzi had told Ahmam's mom, "Ahmam's hands are not for hair washing."

Mom responded, "You liar!"

Kueitzi, who was like a sister to Mom, grabbed Ahmam's hand and showed it to Mom, saying "Ahmam has thick fingertips, and the flesh prevents her nails from growing longer. These kinds of hands will get sore from rubbing scalps after just a short time."

Mom also grabbed Ahmam's hand to check, then she shook her head, sighing. "A princess's body with a servant's fate; it's so hard to raise this kid."

"Ahmam has a wonderful head shape," Kueitzi said when she was drying Ahmam's hair.

"What's the benefit of it? She is too small and can't bear the finer qualities of good outfits." Mom just wanted to criticize Ahmam anyway.

"Ahmam's shape is not bad at all. I don't see any problem with her smallness. You should be satisfied with your children. I couldn't bear any children. A husband is useless—you can't stop them from vanishing away—but children are different. They return for special occasions." Kueitzi was sentimental.

"Don't feel sad. Let's go together to the graves and burn some incense for our husbands sometime." Mom said to comfort her.

When Mom and Ahmam left Kueitzi's place, Ahmam fiddled with her bangs, which she felt had been cut at too short. "Why would you want to change the style they chose for you? I don't understand you. You are so hard to please." Then Mom seemed to see something, she stretched out her hand to brush Ahmam's bangs aside. "You are a big girl now. Don't keep that childish hairstyle. If you keep covering your small face with hair, good luck will never come to you." Ahmam's mother shook her head.

As they walked by a fruit stall, the woman vendor smiled at them. Her golden false teeth showed. She asked, "Is this Ahmam? Married?" "

You fool, did I ever send you wedding cakes?" Mom replied. The woman still smiled happily.

Mom put a bag of tomatoes on the scale, and the woman said: "One hundred." Mom said:

"Aren't you making a mistake? Such a cheap thing can't cost so much."

"Jinju, these are not the tomatoes we are used to eating, they are called Super Saint Virgin—imported."

"What's that supposed to mean? They look about the same as any other tomato just a bit longer. What's a Super Saint Virgin anyway? They don't taste different." Mom grabbed some and wiped them on her own blouse before popping them into her mouth. Juice gushed out as she bit them. Mom put the tomatoes she had selected back to the stall and turned to tell Ahmam, "See, without money, you can't even eat."

"Want some papaya?" the vendor asked.

"No thanks. We grow our own papayas, you know. Maybe I will have some apples though." Mom picked some apples with the shape of five fingers on their bottoms, and she asked Ahmam, "Do you remember we bought an apple like this for your outing when in elementary school?"

Ahmam shook her head. "No, I don't remember." Mom looked disappointed. Why didn't Ahmam admit she remembered? She remembered not only the apple but also the moonlight of that night, as well as her excitement for the apple, which was as magic as Aladdin's lamp. She couldn't sleep that night.

Ahmam asked herself why she could not even share a simple thing like this with her mom. The snake that once attacked her mom was attacking her now; she had no idea it could be so painful. Ahmam's taut expression softened. She turned to her mother, but she was busily selecting apples and engaging in her ritual of complaining about them to the vendor.

Family Rituals

They passed the family shrine, a plastic bag of apples rustled against Ahmam's legs. Kids were yelling, like they were competing against one another, "Nainai, aunty!" Their powerful calls were like drums. "Don't call me 'Nainai' like a mainlander. Call me 'Ahmam' so you will be more like my grandchildren." She stuttered in Mandarin to please the little kids.

Entering the house, Ahmam's youngest older brother had arrived too. She called to him in a low voice and they went into the bedroom. The memories about their playing a long time ago still lingered. She noticed that he still did not like to wear shoes; his feet had turned yellower. They used to stand in two large water tubs a piece, stamping on the preserved vegetables with their body weight. The preservatives made their feet yellow. In those days

Ahmam avoided visiting her classmates who lived in Japanese style houses; she was afraid to take off her shoes in the tatami sitting rooms. One time their teacher took them to a stream, Ahmam resisted taking off her shoes and playing in the water with her classmates.

When Ahmam was in her last year of junior high school, all three of her brothers were attending school away from home, but Ahmam wrote letters to her youngest older brother most often. She even told him that one time she was washing the panties she wore one day before and was frightened to see many ants climbing around the white secretion at the bottom. In school, Ahmam secretly passed a note to her classmate, telling her the story. She said Ahmam must have diabetes because ants liked sweet things. Ahmam thought to herself, I never had candy, how can I have diabetes? By the time her brother wrote her back, telling her not to worry, Ahmam had already begun to worry about something else. Today Ahmam decided not to pass on Lihsiang's regards to him in case he was still sensitive about it.

"It's mealtime; why are you hiding in the bedroom?" Mom called Ahmam out and instructed her two daughters-in-law in cooking. They were all busy. Ahmam stepped to the sitting room, and her youngest older brother was teaching the kids the dance of the fortune god, just like the time he taught Ahmam the same dance during the New Year. At this moment the standing clock by the wall made somber chimes with the pendulum, and

Mom rushed over and hit Ahmam on her shoulder forcefully.

"You are still daydreaming. Hurry up, light the candles and incense. We almost missed the hour; the day is darkening now. If we don't prepare dinner before nightfall, your Dad will be starved. You children did not fulfill your filial duties when your Dad was alive; at least you should hold bowls for him after he died." Ahmam stood up immediately and lit six incense sticks—three for the gods and three for Dad. Dad's memorial tablet was decorated with red flower cuttings. In the middle part was Dad's name with a polite title "Sir Wu" over a white backdrop, the calligraphy was still fresh.

A grandaunt living next door came to borrow some shrimp sauce and garlic, seeing Ahmam arranging her father's altar, she praised her.

Mom replied coldly, "She is like a princess. She never helps if you don't urge her." The comment about Ahmam probably warned her two sisters-in-law; they immediately carried out dishes and soup from kitchen. Mom tested the food they prepared and, not surprisingly, she shook her head like a strict judge.

The kids poured into the room at the same time. They crammed through the door without yielding to one another. Bebe, the youngest, was the first one to lose the battle. She was kicked out. Bebe cried as loud as she could, and Ahmam's Mom shook her head again.

"Use your chopsticks to pick up the chicken first. It represents building a home," Mom advised. Little

Whale and Bebe picked the chicken tail at the same time, and everyone laughed. A gust of wind blew into the house, and one candle Ahmam had just lit was blown out and fell over. Mom noticed Ahmam did not put chopsticks on her dad's altar, she said, "Ahmam, were you unwilling to prepare dinner for your Dad? How can he eat without chopsticks? No wonder the candle fell." Ahmam hurried to put out a pair of chopsticks.

"Sorry, my daughter knows nothing. Please enjoy your dinner." Jinju apologized. She lit the candle again, and the wind circling in the house made the flame surge high. It was the first New Year without Dad. Before this year, no matter how crazy he was gambling, he was around on New Year's Eve. The red wine on the table and the red envelopes after dinner must be presented as if he had been there.

"He was sent to heaven, to be an official in the heaven," Ahmam said. She had made up this story because Mom cried so much after Dad's death, like the tragic actress in the local opera. Ahmam even told Mom that Dad had showed up in her dreams, telling her what he was doing in another world.

To Ahmam's surprise, Mom was convinced by her story. After forty-nine days of mourning, Mom went to the fields to pick bright red cockscomb flowers, yellow sunflowers, and any other kind of white flowers that blossomed during the cooking time each day. She piously offered them at Dad's altar. Ever since that time, the flowers for Dad never stopped. "Your dad is an official now; he must like a more splendid arrangement. These white flowers are suitable for nothing but your dad." Tears oozed from the corners of Mom's eyes when she said this, Ahmam couldn't tell if she was happy or sad. Mom added, "Your dad will bless you and guide you to find a good husband."

Since Ahmam's trip home, the term "a good husband" had continually come to her ears.

"Ahmam, throw the lots to ask if your Dad has eaten." Ahmam stood up to find the two coins on the altar.

The coins covered with smoke from incense were like antiques. Ahmam cast them, and both were negative, landing on the side of the plum flower.

"He must be angry that we even forgot to pre-pare chopsticks for the New Year's Eve Feast. Tell Chung-Jien you are sorry and everyone is back home safely now. And, don't forget to ask him to bless you for a good marriage." Ahmam had to murmur her prayer in front of everyone and cast the coins again. This time there was one negative side and one positive side, so all of them resumed dining.

The New Year's Eve Feast was a family reunion, everyone took turns leaving the table and coming back again. The young mothers chased off to feed their kids, Ahmam's brothers kept answering phone calls, and Ahmam's mom was running between the kitchen and the dining room to add more food or drink. Ahmam was the only one staying at the table, but her mind was far away. Memories of the past year flashed in front of her eyes, and everyone carved a mark of history in her heart: Linzhan, Juchi, and Jiachang. Her love and melancholy were intertwined.

Mom began to ask Ahmam's brothers about any of their single male colleagues who might be suitable for Ahmam. Ahmam did not want to listen, so she excused herself to go play with the kids lighting firecrackers. She took her bowls and chopsticks to the door. Looking out, she knew neighbors and distant relatives were all reunited at their homes; the long history was marked by another year. If it had not been New Year's Eve, a typical winter night in this village was quiet, an absolute quietness.

In the daytime this village was women's territory; they survived their husbands, their children lived in cities, and their long lives were bitter. They farmed small parcels of land to support themselves. Visiting each other was the only entertainment for them. Before the sky turned dark, the mailman's bicycle arrived and they received the mail a little bit late, as usual. The letters usually included money from their children in the cities; they all got such mail.

"Don't live to be as old as I am," Grandma Shou said to Ahmam last New Year. She was in tears, but they were so dry. Grandma Shou was a very old, meager woman. Ahmam wondered if she was still alive. The seashore flooded many times this year, Ahmam thought as she put food in her mouth, absentmindedly. She had been startled to see that Grandma Shou's breasts had dropped to her waist, like two chest pockets. Ahmam couldn't help herself from glancing at her mom's chest. Her plump breasts were still standing tall. Sometimes in the summer, Mom did not put on a top right away after showering. Ahmam was amazed that Mom had such big breasts. It's interesting that in this destitute village, there was a long-lived woman like Grandma Shou and a big-busted woman like Mom.

In the chaos of diseases and poverty, their lives proceeded without missing a beat. The day Ahmam was born, Jinju had to cut the umbilical cord herself. Many villagers who had left home for a long time still remembered Ahmam as "the baby Jinju delivered herself late at night." And others would say "oh, oh," to show their knowledge of this story. Maybe on the night of Ahmam's birth, her mother's shouts of the tearing pain had provided their neighbors with the best materials for their dreams.

And as the life in this village had finally stabilized, all the men raced to their graves like the fastest one was the winner. Ahmam's Dad died at fifty-four. Compared to other men in this village, he had a relatively long life.

Ahmam thought of Chung Jien and the shirt he wore before he passed away.

It was a white shirt printed with the red name of a pesticide, covering Dad's swollen belly. She felt sentimental again.

"Don't eat against the door. Only baggers do that," Jinju shouted to Ahmam.

Aunt Da

Ahmam returned to the table. Jinju picked up a big chunk of fatty pork and dipped it in the garlic-flavored soy sauce before throwing it into her mouth, but it dropped right back out immediately. "I can't bite meat anymore." The anger of not being able to enjoy the food she liked made Jinju shed tears.

"You should not have taken the cheap treatment," Ahmam's oldest brother said.

"You blame the dentist? My bad teeth are because of you guys. The hard labor I did to support my children is the cause of my weak teeth, and now they are beyond any cure." Mom picked up the pork from the floor, the teeth marks on it were stained with blood. No one dared to speak a word then.

The symbolic New Year's Eve Feast was finally done. Jinju stood up and walked to the sitting room to make it clear that she was not going to do dishes. She sat in front of the TV and tried the remote control, but it was not working. "Why did you buy this useless thing? Why not just give me the money?" Everyone alertly presented the red envelopes they had prepared for Mom. At that moment firecrackers were set off somewhere. Ahmam took the remote control to check it and found there was no battery in it. She switched the TV on by pressing the button on the TV set, and the blaring volume of New Year's music almost deafened her.

Jinju once said that the first time she watched a TV was when she was a teenager, she thought it was someone behind the TV playing. She went to check to see who was behind it. Of course she wasn't so silly now; the silly one was her daughter. Why was it that her classmates in college could become triumphant anchorwomen on TV but not Ahmam? She even had a problem supporting herself. Mom often asked, "Can you give me an explanation of why you are not making money? Your ability is no worse than anyone else's, and your looks are not too bad compared to any other girl in this village. Why do you have such a problem surviving?" Mom stretched her finger to check how many bills were in the red envelope from Ahmam, and she asked, "Did you use the money your Dad left you?"

Ahmam was stunned that her mom even suspected it.

"Good." Mom still wondered where Ahmam got the money.

Ahmam decided to take a walk in the village because it was time for the TV news, she predicted Mom would ask her again if any of the anchorpersons had been classmates of hers. Moreover, the scenes broadcast by the mass media annoyed her. She did not want to see anything related to the work she did in the city.

All the kids waited for her while Ahmam put on her shoes. She had to take all o four kids with her for a walk along the ditch surrounding their village. It was quiet, the moon and stars were faint, and blue fog enshrouded the murky night. The low chirping of insects hiding in the seams of ruined bricks were the only sound. The kids began making terrifying sounds. Their shrieks penetrated the woods and were then blown away by the wind.

They approached a small, dimly lit shop by an irrigation ditch, run by Ahmam's oldest aunt on her mother's side. They had to carefully go across a tiny wooden bridge to get there, but Ahmam could only grab one kid at a time, and the others leaped or stomped. Ahmam had to call out "Aunty Da" for help. She was afraid the kids would fall in the ditch like she had so many years ago.

Aunt Da responded by turning on more lights. Though it was a narrow shop, it provided almost everything needed for daily life. On the old-style wicker shelves were displayed several glass jars. The cookies inside were also old-style yellow round crackers decorated with pink sugar flowers.

They inspired the curiosity of the kids, and everyone pressed their nose to the jar to look closely.

Aunt Da's eyesight had regressed, but her hearing was still sharp. She could tell it was Ahmam, although she had problems telling the noisy kids apart. Aunt Da had been an unfortunate woman; her husband was killed a long time ago in the massacre conducted by the government military in Taipei when he went there trying to find a job. The death of her husband left her with a deep, unrecoverable wound.

Aunt Da's son was killed by a speeding truck on an expressway several years ago and his wife took off not long after the accident, leaving the miserable widow and devastated mother with a little baby girl. The villagers said, "It's good that her grandchild is a girl, or some bad thing might happen again. Men are cursed in that family." Aunt Da wished for her daughter Chiuyin to be married, Chiuyin stayed with her. She worked for a bowling club in town and had been approached by matchmakers often, but even the most convincing one, Ahmam's mother, couldn't change her mind.

Looking around the whole place, Ahmam thought to herself, "This place is even bleaker than the fields. It's not like New Year's at all." The bright red couplets attached to the door read: "Great Harvest of Five Grains, Prosperity of All Offspring," which was exactly the opposite of the reality. Nothing except the couplets showed any sigh of the New Year's festivities.

"Where's cousin Chiuyin?"

"She was under the weather, so she went to bed early." Aunt Da said as she happily opened the jars and gave cookies and candies to the children. "Your kids are already so big, Ahmam?"

"They are not mine; they are my brothers' kids." Aunt Da's memories were fading.

Mom once said, "She is losing her mind. She sells a pack of instant noodles for twenty dollars and sells a bottle of soy sauce for five dollars." The kids were quiet as they ate their cookies and candies.

Ahmam took out the red envelope she had prepared for Aunt Da, but she did not want to take it. Little Whale and Bebe fought for the envelope. Bebe lost and began to cry again, and Aunt Da gave them more cookies and candies to calm them down. Ahmam insisted on giving the red envelope to her aunt, saying it was for good luck. Hearing "good luck," Aunt Da accepted it happily and wished for Ahmam to "find a good husband".

What an irony. From the florist to her own family, every woman she met that day seemed to wish for her to "find a good husband," no matter how much they had suffered from their own marriage. This village of widows had shown Ahmam what life could be like in the future.

Aunt Da was dozing off, so Ahmam led the kids away from her stall quietly. When they walked across the small wooden bridge, Ahmam heard her cousin Chiuyin say, "You sleep in the sitting room in such freezing weather; no one would know if you froze to death. Maybe it would be easier to let you die." Ahmam's heart throbbed. She was so surprised that her cousin who used to be a very understanding girl had now become a harsh woman; her tenderness had been eroded by hardship over time. Ahmam regretted the past friendship with her cousin—the hide-and-seek they played in childhood and the romantic ideas they shared as teenagers.

As the kids were walking and playing, little Bebe was behind everyone. She made sounds like weeping every now and then. Bebe always cried for more food, saying "I want to eat! I want to eat…"

One time Jinju said mockingly, "This little kid's previous life must have been that of an African child who died of starvation." Bebe's mother hated that comment, so she refused to bring Bebe back to see her grandmother for quite some time after that.

Looking at greedy Bebe, Ahmam laughed. Earlier when Ahmam gave her the totoro that was almost as tall as she was, she said, "I want to eat! I want to eat!" The responses of children to toys were inexplicable, Ahmam thought. When Ahmam was six, her mom and brothers left her behind in an itinerant flea market because she was utterly distracted by a doll whose head could sway along to the music. The terror of missing her family at that time was still fresh today. That night a vendor who sold drugs for injuries hit his drum and said to Ahmam: "Come with uncle, join the kung Fu society and travel around all the mountains and waters." Ahmam did not understand what she was being invited to do, but she understood it meant to join him and was even more frightened. She cried her heart out so hard that the canopy for the market was on the verge of collapse. She imagined her destiny would be the same as the little monkey kept on a leash by the vendor. Fortunately Ahmam's youngest older brother retraced the path they had taken and found her. Mom made fun of her by saying that if she did not stop crying, she would be sent to another family. The threat made Ahmam cry again. The light bulbs in the market pricked her watering eyes. She became very sleepy and was almost dragged home by Jinju and brothers.

When Ahmam and the four kids returned home, the sitting room was silent Their walk took no more than half an hour; the incense lit on Dad's altar were still burning. Ahmam listened carefully. They were all on the other side of the wall. Mom seemed to be weeping. She walked to the other room. All five adults were sitting around Jinju, and everyone looked grave.

Ahmam wondered what made them so upset, like funeral goers instead of people celebrating the coming of New Year.

"I am being sent to Malaysia by my employer after New Year's, so I can't take care of Mom. I've asked them to take Mom to Taipei and live with them in turns." Ahmam's youngest older brother explained. He had been the one taking care of Jinju since his work on the mountain was not far away from home.

The cigarette butts all over the floor suggested that Ahmam had missed a furious quarrel, probably as agitating as those debates about politics on TV.

Ahmam's sister-in-law, Little Whale's mother, complained that the news should have been brought up earlier so they would not have spent the money on the TV. Ahmam's youngest older brother suddenly got up, lifted the blue curtain, and walked away. His profile reminded Ahmam of Lihsiang. Did her brother decide to leave home because of a regretful relationship?

"How would Mother handle her new situation?" Ahmam asked herself. She always overcame difficulties and she certainly would do so again, Ahmam thought.

First Day of the New Year

In the early morning of the first day of the New Year, Ahmam's mother went to the field she rented from a landowner to pluck some vegetables for the breakfast.

The sounds of a wok and spatula clanging from the kitchen were the premonition of a family storm. The previous night Ahmam had fallen asleep amidst the seemingly endless explosions of firecrackers and woke up realizing it was actually a heavy rain falling on the roof. Now as she woke up, she found she was covered by a flowery blanket, and that by her bed was a wooden bucket that had once been used as a toilet. Ahmam was told she once fell in the toilet bucket when she was little. "Fortunately the urine had just been emptied that night," Jinju had said. Going to the bathroom in such a countryside location was a very troublesome thing. One couldn't avoid being bitten by mosquitoes. Ahmam hated it. She suspected the many mosquito bites and the bad smell from the outhouse let everyone know what she had just done.

Her third aunt's home installed the first flush toilet in the village. Ahmam liked to go to her bathroom, but Jinju felt it was another odd habit of Ahmam's. She always said, "You can release it anywhere when you're working in the fields. I prefer to release mine in the fields." The intolerable smell of the bucket was long gone; now it was more like an antique than a toilet. "What would it be like falling into it now?" Ahmam wondered. Mom called her from the kitchen and nagged that getting up too late in the New Year made her lazy for the rest of the year. She recited a proverb: "Cloudy days are false signs of rain. Lazy people are no better than dead." She added that the energy of every person was limited, so by getting up before; seven one could make the best use of the limited energy. Ahmam thought of the stereotypical saying about the early bird that she had never believed as she got up unwillingly from the warm bed.

Ahmam went to the backyard to take down the basin hung over the wall and got water from the pump to brush her teeth and wash her face. The rain of the previous night wetted the muddy ground, and she knew the sounds of firecrackers she heard now were real because their smoke was blown around by wind gusts. The fresh air of the grass after the rain was gradually overcome by the smell of pickled bamboo sprouts from the kitchen.

Ahmam loved it. The sounds of kids weeping and fighting were heard now and then. Little Whale joined Ahmam to wash, just as unwilling to get up as her. He squeezed toothpaste from his Snoopy tube to brush his teeth. The grave atmosphere was diluted by the kids playing. Ahmam's two brothers actually agreed to take Jinju to live with them in turns, but Jinju did not want to. She said first she wanted to go to Malaysia, then admitted she wouldn't feel comfortable living in Taipei. Ahmam's sisters-in-law suggested that Ahmam should move back to the village to take care of her mom since she couldn't find a well-paying job in Taipei anyway. Jinju's tough personality came back, she said furiously. "Don't just think of yourselves". Ahmam is eventually going to get married. In this village with nothing but old people and small kids, Ahmam's life would be wasted. You want to see her spend her life alone? Without her own family and any money, like me, and die in solitude?" Jinju's remarks outlined the lives of hers and her daughters. She believed despite the differences between their generations and their marital status, they would both end up sharing the same fate. Ahmam was dumbfounded.

Jinju urged Ahmam to change into a new outfit. "We are all going to worship the gods and visit your Dad's grave for the first day of the New Year. I checked his grave yesterday. The weeds grow so fast; they are almost high enough to block his picture. The weeds are too sharp to pull out by hand, and I am too old to cut them now." Facing the light, Jinju was putting on a bright purple dress, which made her tattooed eyebrows looked even darker. Ahmam always drew an association between her mother and the desolate earth she had depended on her whole life.

Visiting Wu Chung Jien

The moisture in the mud was gradually dried by sunlight. The family walked in a single-file line, passing the golden fields of Rapa flowers, like a parade for a wedding. Jinju was in the front, wearing a flowery headscarf and holding a bamboo basket. Ahmam and the kids followed, playing bells and lighting sparklers. The Rapa flowers would be ploughed into the earth in the next spring to fertilize the rice. Ahmam always thought the golden rice tassels had the spirits of those flowers in them when the rice was ready to be harvested. Ahmam was amazed to see field after field of these flowers with their stems connected to each other like a dense net. Lost in such sentimentality, Ahmam told herself to stop her wild imagination about flower spirits or at least to stop pitying herself.

Fewer and fewer graves could be put beside fields nowadays, and as tenant farmers without their own land, Ahmam's family had problems even finding a place to bury their father. The public cemetery quite a distance away was the best place. The thick clouds gathered over the hill, overshadowing it. As they walked to the top, they came upon blackbirds pecking rotten fruit and the corpses of small animals.

The heat was growing. The trees for their father's grave were still too small. Jinju took out cooked pork, fish, and chicken for worship, and the sunlight steamed the meats. A fly rushed down at full speed like a propeller jet, aiming precisely at the chicken. When the fly had almost landed on the chicken tail, Jinju quickly detected it and waved it away with equal precision. Ahmam was stunned, but her mom said regretfully, "Maybe that was Chung Jien's reincarnation. He wanted to take the food we prepared for the New Year, but I brushed him away."

When they were burning money paper, the flame was surging in the wind gusts from the coast, and a small banyan tree's top was devoured by the fire. Ahmam's youngest older brother who had planted the tree the previous year said the banyan was not going to grow any taller since its top was ruined. But he had brought another tree seedling, as tiny as the palm of an adult's hand. The kids squatted around to see it, and Jinju asked what it was. He said something like "heartless stone" and Jinju repeated it, but he said, no, it's not "heartless," it's "black heart stone," Formosan mycelia. Grown Formosan mycelia would be very valuable. Ahmam felt it was difficult to believe that such a small thing could be worth a lot one day.

Jinju observed that the public cemetery was almost full. The population of the deceased was growing fast. When she was young, only a few were buried here. Generations passed like flowing water. "Waking up from a love dream, seeing you away for the final journey, the chilly wind cuts my face, my man, the final departure." The heartbreaking lament contained more grief than the opera tragedy it came from. Ahmam felt her soul was torn apart. She imagined herself as a performer in the tragic opera on a gloomy day, dressed in a costume including a headscarf studded with shinning faux jewelry and a colorful satin dress. As she stepped out into the audience, accompanied by drums and gongs, the stage would be a flood of grief. When the performance was done, she would undress, pack, and watch as the stage was dismantled. Taking off again, her next stop would be wherever she could survive.

"Life is as unpredictable as the sea; no one knows what is going to happen," She would say. Jinju poured rice wine to worship the local god and Chung Jien. Before the incense finished burning, she wanted everyone to peel duck eggs as a symbol of their wish for Chung Jien to be reincarnated soon. The heights of the weeds were about as high as a person's waist. Jinju ordered them to fix this and everyone began to pull or cut them, except

Ahmam. Ahmam felt the weeds and the wildflow-
ers did not want to be gotten rid of, so she stood
and looked on. Jinju nagged her again. She said a
lazy girl would have problems with the family of her
husband in the future.

After they did this, Chung Jien's picture, which
lay on the headstone, was visible again. In it he was
a distinguished man, looking more like a scholar
then a farmer. Ahmam had developed the picture
in a friend's darkroom. In the studio, her tears had
dropped into the liquid developer. Her dad's smile
in the ripples was so dreamy and so unreal. When
Ahmam walked out of the darkroom, she had to
lean on the masonry wall to regain her breath.

After their visit to the grave, thick clouds gathered quickly, threatening to rain. Jinju told everyone
to duck under a plywood canopy for shelter. The
canopy was half-collapsed. If the rain were heavy
it probably wouldn't keep them dry. Fortunately
the shower was short, like a fake gesture of nature.

The golden fields of Rapa flowers were still shiny,
and butterflies accompanied them along the walk.
Mom said in Taipei, dead people were cremated
and their ashes were put in jars and kept in pago-
das, which was against tradition. "Death is equally
important as birth. Your dad spent his life working
on the farms belonging to others; he should at least
have a place to rest after death. You don't have
to worry about your life in the future because your
father took his last breath in the morning. He meant
he was leaving you guys two meals in a day. Had
he passed away in the night, you would have been

left with nothing. Later when you are picking up his bones and reburying him, do not forget to buy him more gold necklaces and rings," Jinju bade them as she was led the group again.

The first time Ahmam bought gold accessories in her life, she was asked by the jewelry store staff, "For whom you are buying these?"

She replied: "For my father." So the woman presented many items with lucky characters, like Blessings, Wealth, Longevity, and Happiness. Ahmam shook her head at all of those and selected one without any pattern. On the day for the ceremony for putting the deceased in the coffin, the daughter was to dress the father. Everyone was to witness Ahmam put the necklace and ring on Dad. It was the most difficult moment of her life. She neared her dad lying in the coffin. The formal suit made him look like a puppet; it was so ridiculously strange to her. Ahmam heard some woman behind her say, "When he was alive, he was never given such luxurious things. What's the point of giving them to him when he is to be buried?" That day Ahmam secretly took a nail used for sealing her dad's coffin as a souvenir. She had no idea why she wanted to do it, but she couldn't help herself.

Ahmam never got any red envelopes from her dad on New Year's. Such business was always in Mom's charge; any of Dad's money was given by Mom. Because Dad had been quiet all his life, Ahmam felt that what he had said to her was especially unforgettable. Dad once gave Ahmam an antique coin he found in the field. What he said at that time was probably the closest thing to a typical father-daughter conversation they ever had. "If it is a real antique, it will be valuable, and it will be your dowry." On the school trip to Taipei during her last year in senior high, Ahmam spent a lot of time browsing ancient coins when they were in a museum but found no clue suggesting the coin from her dad was an antique. Not long afterward, when their home was burglarized, the coin was gone, and the small stereo that had provided entertainment when Ahmam was preparing for college examinations disappeared too.

The family shrine was in sight by that time. Firecrackers could be heard here and there. The tablets of the Wu Family had been brought there from Zhangzhou in China many generations ago. As a woman, Ahmam would not be presented with them. She was not even recorded in the family pedigree. Mom always said: "A girl belongs to her husband's family." Where would she end up? Maybe she really had to be drifting through life with nothing but the simplest of luggage. Ahmam doubted whether it was better to belong to another family; she'd rather never settle down.

Grandma

In the second day of the New Year, Ahmam was sent to visit her grandma. Jinju told her, "Grandma and I are not close to each other because she was not my real mother; that's why you are not adored by her. But as juniors, we must fulfill our filial duties. I know she is not expecting us, she'd rather receive money." Jinju gave Ahmam a red envelope and some red rice cakes she had made. Bebe had already put on her uncle's helmet so she could follow Ahmam out. Jinju saw her small head in the big hat and laughed. "It's like a fly wearing the shell of a longan fruit." Bebe did not know that her aunty was unable to ride a motorcycle. Ahmam took off alone on foot, and Bebe, who was held back by her mother, began bawling. Ahmam envied the freedom of kids being able to cry so wildly and she wished she could release herself like that. Her tears flowed frequently, but she was unable to cry out. She wished her silent agony could be more dramatic, like a child's. In contrast, Mom was still able to wail agitatedly. Although Mom's crying reminded Ahmam of the actresses in cheap performances using truck beds as a stage, she admired her mom's courage in showing her emotions so easily. Jinju was a talented singer; she presented the misery of her life through weeping and storytelling. The phrases she sang were all brimming with sadness, and she was invariably in tears when she was singing such words. But once she has done with her weeping, she could swallow food and drink soup like nothing had happened. The seemingly incurable distress from the moment before was gone like a passing storm. Once when the farming work was less demanding, she was hired to pretend to be the daughter of the deceased and cry professionally at funerals. Grandma was irritated; she felt she was cursed by that job. Jinju said, "I won't drop a tear when she dies. I am not going to cry at her funeral." In acrimony she added, "My own mother left me when I was three. I did not even know she had died. When she was laid under a grass sheet, I lifted the sheet and asked her to feed me milk. My stepmother was only nice to her own children. We couldn't even share the flavors of the good things she gave them. Thinking of this, my blood pressure surges, like it is shooting out in anger." Ahmam walked toward the back of Grandma's house, which was surrounded by old bamboo and windbreak trees. Through the trees Ahmam could see Grandma chewing betel nuts on her way home from the field. Her bent backbone and bare feet did not slow her agile steps at all; she looked like those old women with high martial arts skills in kung fu movies. Ahmam was amazed. When Ahmam arrived at her door, her Grandma was chopping wood. She did not say Ahmam's name, she just greeted her and told her to sit in the living room. Ahmam stepped across the gate. Grandpa's worship tablet on the altar faced her. Grandpa adored Ahmam a lot. He once rode his bicycle to the melon trellis where little Ahmam was hanging about and gave her a pair of small wooden sandals he made. One New Year when he knew that Ahmam's mom was not going to his home, he rode his bicycle to their house and delivered little Ahmam a string of coins he had tied with red thread. The coins couldn't be used to buy candies; they were made from Japanese money. Grandpa died during the devastating typhoon. He had already lost his mind by that time and did not know he should run when the water began flooding into his house. Grandma was engaged in bringing her kids up to the roof. By the time she wondered about her husband, Grandpa had been devoured by the waves. Grandpa's pale and swollen body wasn't discovered until the typhoon receded and the flood withdrew. And the coins he had given Ahmam also disappeared, as Ahmam's room was destroyed and her things also washed away. Ahyong, her uncle's son, walked out to the sitting room, carrying a bowl of rice. He greeted Ahmam and sat beside Grandma.

Ahyong had entered senior high school last autumn. He was a bashful boy. The grandma and the grandson were attached to one another very deeply. Even at Jinju's home they could hear Grandma's shrieking calls to Ahyong through the windbreak forest. Jinju commented sourly, "You can hardly lose such a big boy. The reason she calls to him so eagerly is to let everyone know she has a treasured baby." Ahmam realized that the energy she saw from Grandma just now came from her care of her Grandson. She wondered if there was spontaneous vitality in the mutual dependence of the two. Ahmam sat for a while. She took several bites of the not-very-juicy sugar canes they grew, and she was still ill at ease. Then Ahmam took out the red envelope Jinju prepared, but Grandma did not want to accept it. The air was frozen. Ahmam decided to put it at Grandpa's altar and turned to leave. She expected Grandma would chase her to return the envelope immediately, but she heard no steps. Ahmam now understood that Grandma just felt embarrassed to take the money from her. Walking toward home, Ahmam saw her steps leave clear marks in the muddy ground. She began paying attention to every mark she left, and her attention made each footprint into an orderly arrangement. The walk reminded her of the pilgrimage to the town she had conducted with friends during her teenage years. It took at least one hour to walk to the town, Ahmam loved the solid feeling of walking on the paths. Sometimes the military trucks roared past her, and the soldiers would whistle, inviting her to ride with them, but Ahmam turned them down. She enjoyed her relaxing walk. The big houses of rich families in town had been vacated by their owners a long time ago. Ahmam and her childhood mates used to climb up the trees to look at their yards. They made up stories about the many wives of rich men or stayed in the shade of banyan trees to listen to the old man telling stories about the Jiaching Emperor's expedition in Taiwan. Ahmam imagined herself as the girl the emperor encountered and fell in love with. She wrote down the characters for "Jiaching Emperor" on almost every margin of her textbooks. When Ahmam was preparing for examinations in college absentmind-edly in the corridor of an ancient private school, she found a worn-out plaque hung over the gate. Upon it was carved "Lunar April, Year of Kuei-Yuo, the Reign of Jiaching." Ahmam threw down her English grammar book and ran to the old man tak-ing a nap under the banyan tree and shook him awake. Ignoring the fact that she had shocked the old man into a cold sweat, Ahmam yelled excit-edly, "It's real, it's real! He was really here!" Ahmam suddenly realized that this was the year of Kuei-Yuo again. They were encountering each other again after centuries apart? Who she was waiting for? Ahmam's heart throbbed a bit, and her mouth slightly opened. "Hello." The voice of a tall man pulled her back from her wild imagination. Why was it that each time they met Ahmam had to be in a peculiar situation? She was called upon by her mother to complete a mission in the early morning.

She had not even had time to wash her face. The last time they met like this many years ago, she was so unprepared. Now she was unprepared once again.

Tsungyin

Tsungyin was Ahmam's short-term lover between boyfriends. Ahmam hated to recollect such a short-lived, transitional affair, but she couldn't deny that they had a connection because Tsungyin was from the same village and they went to the same elementary school. Tsungyin was a short, skinny boy. That's why Ahmam did not recognize him in bustling eastern Taipei where she was temporarily hired to give away sanitary pad samples in the street. He was much taller now. It was easy for Tsungyin to recognize Ahmam because she had only grown fifteen centimeters taller since they left elementary school, and her small face had changed very little. At first, Ahmam thought he must be one of those boys approaching her to ask for free sanitary pads for his girlfriend, so she gave him a whole pack to embarrass him. He smiled. "I have no use for it, Full Score Ahmam." She fixed her eyes to watch him carefully. Only her elementary classmates called her that name.

"Dragonfly Tsungyin!" she said surprised. Tsungyin suggested he could help her hand out the samples, but girls avoided taking sanitary pads from a man. He was serving in the military now. Tsungyin's hair was shaved closely to his scalp, just like when he was in elementary school. He was a naughty but straightforward boy.

One time he grabbed Ahmam's braid to tease her. Outraged, Ahmam lifted her school bag to hit his head. His hurt expression reminded her that there was an ink stone in her bag. He stared at her in confusion and rubbed his head, which had already begun swelling. Later his revenge was sticking chewing gum in her hair. Ahmam was so scared, she wept, believing that all her hair would have to be cut off. Their teacher only had to trim a lock of her hair to get rid of it. She comforted Ahmam by touching her head tenderly, saying, "Don't worry, it's all right now." The punishment for Tsungyin was one hour of standing in class.

The surprise encounter of the two old classmates brought them closer together. They spent the night together to catch up on what had happened after they left elementary school. He went to senior high school in Taipei, and during their college days and his time in graduate school, they had both been in Taipei but never ran into each other until now. They were in Ahmam's place on the roof. The TV was playing *The Deer Hunter*, and the two old acquaintances began making love when Meryl Streep and Robert De Niro reunited. When the sorrowful music ended, Tsungyin ejaculated. It was a short round of lovemaking, and the memory of it to Ahmam was more about the sound track of the movie than their intimate activities.

Ahmam still remembered that when he entered her body and moved up and down, an image flashed in her mind. She saw the two of them becoming fossilized after the world collapsed, a sculpture of two naked bodies. Or perhaps it looked more like one small fish was being devoured by one big fish, but the flesh of both fishes had been eroded; only their bones were left. That night Ahmam realized she could sleep with a man just because she was lonely. When Tsungyin's vacation from military was over, Ahmam went with him to the train station. They dined in the food court at the station first, but Ahmam's stomach ached after eating the fried oysters. Tsungyin bade her to stay as he ran out to find medication for her. Ahmam waited for him for a long time. When Tsungyin finally came back, sweating and panting, her stomach was no longer aching, and the train he was scheduled to take had gone. He did not find any pharmacy until he walked to New Park, which was a whole block away from the railway station. When Tsungyin got on to the next train, his hands still held the medication bag he had bought for Ahmam. She had to pull the bag from him with force. The paper bag was soaked with Tsungyin's sweat; he must have been very nervous. After breaking up with Linzhan,

Ahmam tried many things to recover. She chanted Buddhist scriptures and went to fortune-tellers. One time when Tziyang accompanied her to see a fortune-teller, the fortune-teller said that Ahmam was trapped by love after only taking a glance at her.

Tziyang said eagerly: "Master, you've got to save her!" The master did not say any more words; he just handed Ahmam two pamphlets of Buddhist scriptures. In the difficult days without Linzhan, Ahmam often fell asleep with the two pamphlets and their red covers. Her hands were dyed red when the red paint became imprinted upon her sweaty hands.

Almost the next day after Tsungyin's return to the military, Ahmam received his letter. He wrote in the first sentence "Dearest Chun-Mam, receiving this letter I hope you will feel like you are seeing me in person."

Ahmam felt funny. The letter ended with, "The Buddha said you and me are lovers." Ahmam was touched. He was an engineer who often thought like a machine, so it was quite unusual for Tsungyin to notice that Ahmam had some Buddhist scriptures in her drawer. Nevertheless, such romantic interactions did not last.

At first Tsungyin criticized Ahmam, saying that her work for the movies was little more than acting like a maid, and he was unhappy that every time they went out he had to pay for both of them. When he began complaining that Ahmam was too short, Ahmam realized their relationship was about to end. One time when they went back to their hometown together, he called her the next day, telling her he wanted to break up with her. Though Ahmam had expected it, she was still agitated and insisted they should meet to make things clear.

Ahmam found an excuse to send her mother away, she put on some makeup and dressed up to meet with Tsungyin. He arrived by bicycle. His jean legs were stained with the oil of his bicycle chain, and Ahmam could tell he seemed to be in a big hurry. Tsungyin hesitatingly explained that his ex-girlfriend had returned. She was from his university, majoring in economics, several years his junior. They ran into each other at a car show; she now worked as a model for a car company. Their reunion made Tsungyin realize that he was still in love with her. Ahmam concluded that Tsungyin's ex-girlfriend had a perfect shape, matching his height better. Ahmam did not say a word. She just turned to enter her home and heard Tsungyin's bicycle take off behind her. In the midday sunlight, the shadow of her own stout figure made Ahmam feel every step was heavy.

The worse thing was, Jinju actually saw the whole scene while hiding in the bamboo woods and made the whole thing an endless business instead of letting it remain private. In the following years, Jinju liked to ask every now and then, "Are you still in touch with Tsungyin?" It was really quite natural since Tsungyin was the only one of Ahmam's boyfriends that Mom knew about. Knowing that Ahmam was not seeing him, she always said, "It doesn't matter. He must be a heartless man, dating you without marrying you. He must look down at us farmers. You'll have no problem finding a better man." Mom must have assumed it hurt Ahmam a lot, but Ahmam actually recovered fast, especially when she heard from friends that when his taxi-driver father gave him a ride, Tsungyin asked his father to drop him off one street away from the university's gate so his fellow students would not know how his father made a living.

But the real reason Ahmam was able to forget about Tsungyin easily was her past with Linzhan. She only wondered how she and Tsungyin had gotten together in such a bad situation and at such a low point in her life. It must have been the loneliness bringing them together. On top of that, Ahmam also began to become conscious of the triggering of her childhood memories. Her memories about Tsungyin in their childhood were actually about Ahmam's father. Before Aunt Da's stall was set up, the business of Tsungyin's family was the only store in their village, and shopping there was one of Ahmam's daily errands. Each day Chung Jien consumed one pack of cigarettes, two packs of betel nuts, one vitamin B drink that he liked to mix with rice wine, and some herbal medicine wines. He rummaged in his pants pocket and took out a transparent plastic bag he used to carry receipts, his driving license, ID card, and several small paper bills. He took the bills out and sent Ahmam to buy these things for him. If Jinju knew about it, she'd make a big fuss by banging the wok with her spatula and shouting, "You should drink urine till you die!" Chung Jien still squeezed the money into Ahmam's hand and told her secretly, "You can keep the change." Ahmam tried hard to memorize what she was told to buy and prayed that Tsungyin was not in the store. But he was always in the store, having his dinner with his eyes fixed on the cartoons playing on TV unaware that there was rice on his face. When Ahmam approached, he did not move his eyes from the TV. He just routinely asked what she wanted with his shrill voice. Ahmam did not answer; she looked at the fish tank, and Tsungyin realized it was Ahmam, so he took out the items she always bought for her father. Ahmam said to herself, "He must think my Dad is an alcoholic." The most embarrassing part was giving the payment and taking the change. They avoided touching each other's hands, therefore the coins dropped easily. One time some coins rolled under the glass shelf, through the displayed candies and cookies, Ahmam watched Tsungyin climb on the floor and stretch his hand to reach the money. His face twisted when it pressed against the glass. The accident calmed down Ahmam's excitement at earning change from her dad. Once Ahmam complained to Jinju "The whole village watches me taking wine home every day." Jinju gave Chung Jien a harsh glance and told him, "If you want alcohol, go get it yourself. Don't make your poor daughter a joke in our village." Ahmam wondered if her dad's drinking all day for so many years was because of his loneliness, or the other way around. After her dad's death, Ahmam realized that her dad probably preferred not to be a human being if he couldn't enjoy cigarettes and alcohol. How long had Ahmam been shopping for her dad? She remembered the last time she was in Tsungyin's family store, almost all the fish in the tank were dead. Only the trash fish were still around, and they grew as big as arowanas. Later, Tsungyin's family closed the store. Tsungyin was angry, so he poured the fish tank in a ditch to release his regret that he would no longer be able to show off his unique status as the snack provider in school. he was also no longer able to tease Ahmam with this unique status. Aunt Da opened her stall around that time. Ahmam's dad got a discount shopping there.

Running into Tsungyin during the New Year, Ahmam was surprised that the memories emerging in her mind were about Chung Jien instead of their affair. A sudden gust of wind blew Ahmam's hair up, it carried with it a girl's delicate voice calling," Where is my darling dragonfly?" As she approached she did not bother to find out who Ahmam was, she just pulled Tsungyin away. Tsungyin allowed himself to be pulled forward. He turned without saying good-bye to Ahmam, he just waved his hand behind him. Ahmam could tell that the girl could not be the girl Tsungyin had spoken of when he had broken up with Ahmam that day on his bicycle. It was hard to believe that this man had once proposed to marry her. It was the first proposal in Ahmam's life. He used his pay from the military to buy a bottle of perfume for Ahmam, the first perfume she had received in her life. There were many "first times" between them, but all were gone with the wind by then.

Great Aunt San

It was past noon when Ahmam walked home, the fragrance of High Mountain Green Tea greeted her. Great-aunt San was in their sitting room. She was seventy-five now, and except for the fact that her feet were a little bit swollen, she was in very good shape. Great-aunt San learned to drive a car and got her driver's license at sixty years of age; even now she was still able to drive to town by herself. Ahmam admired her strong will.

When Great-Uncle Wei was executed, Jinju had just married Ahmam's father; Great Aunt Sans was shocked by the incident and did not recover from the horror for a long time. It left a deep scar on the whole village. It was during a time when many of the village males disappeared or were killed after secret arrests. Great-uncle Wei was carried by his wife, using the only bicycle in the village, to the mountains to hide. Great-aunt San never revealed her husband's whereabouts even when policemen pistol-whipped her. The police found Great-uncle Wei after they followed her great-aunt on her way to deliver food to him. They chased him and shot him to death right before her eyes. Witnessing the murder of her husband, Great-aunt San dropped the rice she had brought for him. She had to watch helplessly as her husband lay dying. She was imprisoned for a year on Huo Shao Island for hiding a "political criminal." Two elementary teachers who were the couple's very closest friends and had helped them during Great-uncle San's escape were with her in confinement. After her release, Great-aunt San raised her four kids alone.

Ahmam had only discovered her aunt's history in recent years because no one in her village wanted to talk about it. Ahmam always knew that something terrible must have happened to her Great-aunt her life story couldn't be as plain as that of an ordinary countrywoman. As Ahmam stepped into the sitting room, she heard her mom say, "If I were you, I wouldn't give him a cent. Hasn't your family suffered enough because of him?" She was chewing on melon seeds while talking to Great-aunt San. Curious about what they were discussing, Ahmam made tea for them and hung around. "He was pathetic" Jinju continued. When the thing exploded, he and his communist comrades hid in the field. They slaughtered a sheep to eat. It was a long time before they finally had a chance to board a ship heading for China. He was very ill at that time. He also had his own family to support. I can only explain the fate of my poor Silkworm by thinking that he was unlucky," her great aunt countered. Silkworm was Great-uncle San's nickname. He was the best-educated man as well as the best silkworm raiser in their village. His charismatic personality interested the underground communist organization; he was absorbed into the group and given the rank of director of one branch. It was a crime at that time, and one almost could be sure that, once arrested, it was going to be the death penalty. Ahmam recalled the pictures of Great-uncle Wei she had seen before. Decades apart from his time, his heroic stories were romantic to Ahmam. She told herself, "He tried to find a way out for this barren village but failed." "At that time, the lives of others could be traded for your own. Survival was the only thing anybody fought for. Every survivor deserves respect, Jinju, whether we are suffering or not depends on how we look at ourselves. No matter what happened, I am grateful." Great-aunt San peeled a tangerine carefully while speaking to Ahmam's mother. "Even if you are right about survival, you don't have to give a thousand dollars to a man who was responsible for your husband's death." "The thing has passed like a cloud in the sky. I don't mind it anymore." Her aunt quietly remarked. When Great-aunt San was chewing her tangerine, her wrinkled face wrinkled even more, like an old baby. She added, "I have also made mistakes. If I could not be forgiven, well, that's real suffering." Ahmam guessed the mistake

Great-aunt San meant was her unequal love of her sons. She only loved her younger son and was very harsh to her older son without any clear reason. Feeling treated unfairly, the older brother began having visions of killing his younger brother. Great-uncle Wei once advised her, "You should not treat your kids differently. You never can foretell who will be a better person in the end.. You never know who will fulfill their duties of taking care of you until they decide what kind of woman they will marry." Great-aunt San -eventually changed her attitude toward her sons. This old story Ahmam learned from gossip passing between her great aunt's neighbors.

Great- Uncle Wei was proven right. The wife of Great-aunt San's older son was really close to her. As if it had happened just by thinking of her, the daughter-in-law turned up at their door. Great-aunt San called her in. "Come in Hsinfen she said, join us in some tea Ahmam made. It's a rare opportunity." Everyone turned to look at Ahmam. Aunt Hsinfen took the teacup handed to her and replied. "Sure". "The tea picked and made by young girls tastes better," She continued, "Ahmam never gets older; she still looks like a teenager." "Aunty San, your daughter-in-law is so nice. Ahmam beamed. Her praise only shows how talented she is." I wish Ahmam was as Hsinfen describes, but in fact Ahmam has the mind of an old man," Jinju quickly added. Hsinfen cast a glance at Ahmam while adjusting her teacup. They had tea and chatted a while longer, then Aunt Hsinfen invited everyone to worship Goddess Matzu at the temple of the New

Street. The group of women took off and walked together. Their laughter danced with the dust their steps blew up. Ahmam was intrigued by the open charm that usually seemed so veiled in the village women before.

In the days following the New Year holidays, Ahmam walked to the fields to pick flowers for her dad's altar as her mom requested. Sometimes she was told to cook some minced pork and noodles for her dad too. The rest of the days Ahmam often sat by the sea watching the tides advancing and withdrawing, the sun rising and setting. She recalled the fun she had when reading comic books or romance novels with friends at the same place. Nothing disturbed her, her mind was engaged by nothing.

Tziyang called several times, sharing her experiences of meeting with men her relatives arranged for her. Many of them had degrees from America like her and one of them she actually knew when she lived there. "It's so annoying. I took so many turns and ended up at the same place. This guy is not normal. He is out of his mind. But when I turned him down, my relatives blamed me for setting my standards too high. They'd rather marry me off to a lunatic than see me stay single."

Yingdan spent the whole holiday with the family of her cabbie boyfriend. They played mah-jongg and ate all day. My face has grown even rounder. She said, "I did not know this mellow guy could become such a serious gambler the moment he sat at a mah-jongg table." But it never changed her devotion to him. She asked Ahmam if she was doing fine and Ahmam told them both she was all right.

Jinju and her female relatives went to offer incense at different temples. When the times were difficult, it was the happiest thing for them to do. They took a fifty-minute bus ride to Beikang, where the large Matzu temple was located. Pilgrims gathered there from everywhere. If Jinju had some money, she'd bring sugared peanut brittle or horse beans back with her.

The temple was always crammed with worshippers, Jinju's blouse was often burned by the incense held by the people behind her, she was unaware of it.

Jinju always said, "Goddess Matzu in Beikang shelters people away from home. Since the goddess guards people far away, she certainly guards the village right next to Beikang." No matter how harsh the days were, Jinju always offered incense to this temple, sometimes she even joined the incense-offering tour for Goddess Matzu. Ahmam knew her mom prayed to the goddess to find her a husband every time. Jinju even consulted a fortune-teller about Ahmam's marriage. Ahmam asked her, "You don't even remember the exact hour of my birth, do you? How can a fortune-teller tell my fortune without the precise time of my birth?"

"The fortune-teller can tell what will happen to you by using a piece of your clothing, so I took a shirt you wore when you were in college."

"My god," Ahmam muttered. Her mom had been shrewd all her life, but she could never imagine such a superstitious fortune-telling plot. Ahmam thought to herself, "Everyone has a weakness." Ahmam also realized that she was her mother's major weakness and her mom was hers.

On the fifth day of the New Year, Jinju was hanging clothes to dry in the sun while Ahmam was raking the leaves in their yard. "Ahmam, it's said even a bad husband could be relied on for a whole life time. Don't set your standards too high." Her mom advised once again. "It's impossible to rely on a man for your whole life," Ahmam replied. "Even a good man is not reliable for a whole lifetime, not to mention a bad one."

"You are almost thirty. One day when I close my eyes and leave you forever, whose shoulders can you lean on?" Jinju flopped the wet clothes, water dripped on Ahmam's face, its coolness was soothing. Who was she leaning on? Ahmam smiled without having an answer.

"Your dead ancestors would still worry about your marriage."

Ahmam said to herself, "I have my own way." They heard firecrackers from somewhere off in the distance to celebrate the opening of a market for the New Year. Jinju bade her that they should worship the God of Heaven at midnight exactly. The hour was important, or else the worship would be useless.

"Do you remember the day I took you to get your ears pierced? You cried so much. It was the ninth day of the second month of the lunar year. I remember it clearly because I was told that if we got an ear piercing that day, a girl would have a blessed life...but it never happened to you... probably your ears were too small, like the ears of a mouse." Jinju's remark reminded her of a story Ahmam's friend told her. In Japan, there was a cave hole called Conjugal Hole, girls praying for good marriages would have their dreams come true if they walked through the hole. But an obese girl got stuck in the hole when she tried to pass through it. People behind her had to push her. Ahmam thought of Yingdan and she couldn't help but laugh out loud.

Jinju was confused with her daughter's response to her memory.

The totoro doll's yellow skin had turned dark green after being dragged by the kids for several days. One time they threw it up in the air and it stuck between some tree branches. All the kids stood there looking up without knowing what to do. Ahmam found a bamboo stick to push the Totoro off, when it dropped, the kids cheered.

She also had been trapped in a tree branch once. Many years ago, she climbed up the tallest tree in their village. The screaming of the cicadas there made Ahmam feel she had seen everything possible in life. When she was in college, she watched the movie *Floating Weeds* by Yasujiro Ozu, an experience of listening to cicadas was in the movie.

Ahmam asked Tomomi about the director once, but Tomomi was too young to know who he was.

The five days of the New Year holidays were almost gone, but they never reached any conclusion about where their mother should stay. Ahmam walked with her brothers and their families to the street as they were departing and the temperature suddenly dropped. She walked gloomily on the narrow path, thinking that all the fallen leaves would become a part of the muddy roads eventually. Fates were funny. Many women in this village were widows; some of them had lost their children too, or their children had left them. For those few lucky enough to have their families with them, experiencing poverty as tenant farmers was an unbreakable curse forever. Residents often complained that the feng shui of the village was inauspicious. However, dead people here were not cremated. They said the deceased wouldn't rest unless they could smell the fragrance of the earth. They seemed to forget the hardship they had endured on the land.

Many farmers who owned their own land spent their later years as customers of brothels. Their soiled hands rubbed the breasts of the women serving them. The painted nails of their fingers did not remind those wealthy landowners of their days spent farming, and they chose to turn their eyes away from the more truthful parts they had experienced. Whenever Ahmam walked past the brothels, she was enraged. "These people owned the land but they didn't own much wisdom." Ahmam thought of her childhood friend, Hsiaomam, when she saw Hsiaomam's mother several days later, she inquired where Hsiaoman lived. "Vienna." Hsiaomam's mother replied. "It's a good city, isn't it? Just quite far away from Taiwan." Ahmam said. "No, it's not far away, just two streets from here". Hsiaomam's mother replied. "If you go there, she could give you a discount." Ahmam then understood that "Vienna" was a place for karaoke, not the city in Europe.

Ahmam lifted her face. The sky could be used as the background of a movie. The direction of the wind gusts suggested that a thundering spring was approaching. Insects hibernating in the seams of rocks were waiting for the exchange of cold and warmth when the thunder hit. They were ready for a new life.

Ahmam imagined how her roommates would kill their time on the boring ride to Taipei. Tziyang would probably read a book and Wingding would take a nap. Lihsiang's roommate Chunlang would sing with her boyfriend in his pickup truck, "You are the needle, I am the thread, we shall never go apart..." And the mattress they brought home had to be brought back to Taipei again still, leaping up and down on the bumpy road.

Ahmam also wondered if the red flowers she had bought for Tziyang still blossomed with the good feng shui that Tziyang wished for.

Ahmam imagined that there would be several messages on her answering machine when she got home. One of them would be the match the florist mentioned before. Ahmam wished such matches could be made for her mother too. She wished she hadn't been so scared and ran away when the Mainlander went to find her mother in their village. What could this man have brought her mother? Happiness or an even more difficult time?

Ahmam admired the wisdom her Great-aunt San has demonstrated in her life. The past was like clouds floating by. Ahmam asked herself where she should go.

Replacing A Lost Identity

The sixth day of the New Year, stores and organizations reopened. Jinju urged Ahmam to apply for a reissue of her ID card that she had lost. "Get it done quickly. Jinju scolded. You will need it to apply for jobs. You lost your purse right before the New Year. The person who found it must have felt like they were given a red envelope by you." Ahmam knew if her troubles were known by Jinju, she'd nag her endlessly.

Ahmam lost her purse before she had gone home. Before taking off, Ahmam had dialed Linzhan's number at a pay phone. When Ahmam heard him say: hello from the other end, she felt her throat tighten.

"Ahmam?"

"Hey." Ahmam couldn't speak up. She took a deep breath but felt she was on the verge of

231

crying. The coins she had thrown in the slot were falling one by one as the time passed.

Ahmam finally pulled herself together and said, "Nothing, I just wanted to say Happy New Year to you. How are you doing?" "Fine, I am fine."

"I probably won't be able to return your money soon."

"Forget about it. He said in an unconcerned voice.

Ahmam could no longer control herself. She said good-bye to Linzhan before she burst out crying. She cried for a long time in the telephone booth. When she was finally able to walk out of the booth, it was midnight. The moon has sunken behind the clouds, but she was glad that no one was around to witness her crying. But Ahmam forgot to pick up the purse she had taken into the telephone booth with her. What a costly "Happy New Year" call.

The village office had distinguished dark blue walls, and there were several bicycles parked under the listless betel trees. Pushing open a green door, Ahmam saw people already crammed around the small windows, inquiring about birth, marriage, death, property transfer, or disputes over inheritance. Ahmam approached one window and asked directly: "Miss, what should I do if I lost my ID card?" She had applied for her student loan in this office when she was in her junior year. She had stolen her dad's stamp and their residential registry to complete the procedure. That time there were also many people here. That time, Ahmam had to wait for a long time, and when it was her turn, the middle-aged woman at the counter took a look at her and threw her documents aside, saying, "You can't have student loan until you turn twenty years old. Next in line!" she shouted. The next person approached, but Ahmam was anxious, she yelled: "I am over twenty!" The woman looked at her again and checked her photo on the document, not really convinced. That woman was not here today. Maybe she got a promotion in the intervening years. The young woman at the counter handed her a form to fill out, but Ahmam had a problem filling in the exact date of her mother's birthday. She hesitated for several seconds, then decided to make up some numbers. The woman told Ahmam they still need the ID card and stamp of one of her immediate relatives. Ahmam did not have them, so she called her mother. Jinju complained about how Ahmam should have called the office in advance and complained that being Ahmam's mother was more like being a slave. She had to serve her daughter even in her old age. But she promised she'd bring the things to her by bicycle. In just a few moments, Jinju showed up on a child's bicycle. Her stout body over the small, creaky thing constituted a very funny but amicable scene. Seeing the tires were pressed flat by Jinju's weight, Ahmam laughed. "I work like your maid and you are laughing!" They entered the office again. Ahmam looked at Jinju's ID Card and secretly changed the date she put on the form. It's good that Mom did not read, or she'd nag Ahmam again for not knowing her own mother's birthday.

When they left the office, mother and daughter walked home, pushing the bicycle. The wind was sandy and smoky. Someone was burning trash and weeds in the public cemetery. The celebration of New Year was gone, except that several kids were still playing with bee firecrackers. The shrieking plastic bees seemed to retain the last moments of the holidays. Jinju suddenly said, "When you were a little kid I took you on business with me into town without considering that you were too young to walk so much." Ahmam's heart throbbed. She did not know her mother actually felt guilty about it. "Your father's big brother came to me to borrow some money before the New Year; what an unusual thing. But how can I have money? Furthermore, why does this man have the guts to borrow money? He never worked in the field a day in his life; he never dipped one hand or one leg in the soil." Ahmam smiled. Her mother's memories were like wheels, once activated, they never stopped. "Not long ago I went to the farmers' credit corporation, and the girl serving at the counter asked me if I was paid for my farming work. She was so silly. I asked her how I could I get paid. She said, from your husband.' In this village, women of my generation were mostly widows. When our husbands died we couldn't raise enough money to bury their bodies. Even our tears were exhausted. Your uncle has had a long life because he only had to sell his farm to support his family. People in this village were either murdered by the government, died of hard work, or were killed in merciless natural disasters. Your dad, though, died because of his unrestrained drinking. Compared to the situations of others, I guess we really don't have much to complain about." When Jinju was around, Ahmam's world was never silent. Ahmam listened to her mom, and when she lowered her head to look at her feet and her mother's feet, she wanted to ask her where she planned to stay after the New Year holidays. But once Ahmam lifted her head and saw the determined contours of Jinju, she swallowed her question. Jinju would find her own solution. Her big feet with peeled skin were evidence that she still walked like a tiger and had no problem finding her own path.

Ahmam felt ashamed about her own feet now. They were short with weak muscles. When they walked by a sugar cane field, Jinju told Ahmam the biggest dream she had during her teenage years was to taste the juicy sugar cane. One time she stole a cane in a field and got busted by the farm owner. The man violently lifted her skirt, trying to take advantage of her. She used the cane to hit his private parts as hard as she could and ran away. "It was audacious to steal sugar cane.'" She told Ahmam, "there were some things in life I should have known but was never told because I didn't have a mother to take care of me." Ahmam was impressed by her mother's confession.. Each trip home, Ahmam actually learned a lot about life from her mother.

Home at Last

Yindang called to say she was bored staying alone in Taipei for the previous three days. "Three days? Why did you go back to Taipei so early?" Ahmam asked.

"My boyfriend and I saw the notice that our area would have a water outage for two days, we thought we'd better come back early to store some water. But it did not happen; there was water the whole time. I used all the buckets at home to carry water and now we have way too much water." Yindang told Ahmam their car got a flat tire on their way to Taipei and she was asked to push the car because, as her boyfriend put it, "You ate too much during the holidays." Ahmam laughed at Yindang's addiction to food. Tziyang also called. She was reading horoscope books and decided she should take a trip to the islands in Southeast

Asia because her horoscope indicated that by resting under palm trees she would gain something she always wanted.

Around noon Lin Jinju handed Ahmam a cup of tea, telling her it was good for her health. When Ahmam hesitated, her mom added, "Would I poison you? It's good. Drink it." Ahmam took a sip, the tea tasted a little bitter.

Ahmam saw there were still some sticky rice cakes in their bamboo basket. They had cracked a bit in dry air. She felt sorry for Lin Jinju. It would take a long time for one person to consume them all, and her mom could never throw food away.

Ahmam took a walk as night fell. As she walked near the gardenia garden where she and her childhood playmates had liked to pick the flowers for their fragrance, she saw a lot of people gathered there. Jinju was also in the crowd. They seemed to be waiting for something with a great deal of concentration. Jinju's face looked flushed. They were standing around a Madagascar Almond tree, a very old village tree. Ahmam had learned the tree's name from one of her older brothers. The leaves of the tree would turn bright red before falling; Ahmam imagined it contained the spirit of a beautiful girl who danced until all her blood ran out. This colorful tree probably was the only thing left of value in the destitute village. Her grandma once said when she had just gotten married, both the tree and herself were like juveniles, but now she was old and dying and the tree was still radiating real beauty, which saddened her grandma.

At home there was a picture of Grandma when she was fourteen. Her wonderfully beautiful youth only served as a reminder that a woman's beauty was a quickly vanishing asset. Grandma did not interact with Ahmam's part of the family very much. Mom said her stepmother was a heartless woman. She never even paid her a visit after her difficult delivery of Ahmam when she was on the edge of death.

Standing beside the group of people, Ahmam gradually learned that they were told the tea made from the leaves of the Madagascar Almond tree was very good for the liver. The one condition for getting the desired health benefit being that it was only from the fallen leaves that this worked. Leaves plucked from branches wouldn't do the trick. That's why everyone lifted their faces upward, waiting with outstretched arms for any leaf to flutter from the branches. And when they missed the leaves, they'd bend to pick them up from the ground, bumping into each other in the chaos. Ahmam smiled and decided to sit and watch. Jinju assumed she was about to leave for Taipei, so she rushed toward her and squeezed a handful of the leaves she had grabbed into Ahmam's hands and said, "Two leaves can make a pot of tea. Don't waste it. Drink it while it is still warm. It will make you look pretty and a pretty Ahmam will find a good husband." She then asked, "Why do you go to Taipei so early? You don't have a job… perhaps you should go early so you can find a better job this year. No, stay longer, I cooked chicken in wine this afternoon. The chicken is good, raised on an open range, not like those in Taipei, raised in tiny cages. They, Ahmam assumed she meant the Taipei chickens, become poisonous from a lot of antibiotics their raisers feed them." She turned to look at the crowd and said to Ahmam nervously, "I should pick more, or they will leave me nothing." And she was off.

One time a direct-sales business drove a big truck to their village, Jinju heard about it from the village speakers but figured it must be a scheme to fool countryside people. When she learned the business was giving away free presents, however, she joined them immediately. Jinju took back two cheap plastic stools after hours of standing in line. Her legs had gone numb. That's how competitive she is.

Looking at the leaves in her hand, Ahmam was deeply moved by the energy she saw in her mother. She decided not to go back to Taipei. But what could she do here? The fields had gone desolate. As Ahmam walked back to the wood shack farm her mom rented, the fresh smell of green vegetables overwhelmed her. As she took a hoe to plough the soil she realized that her hands were better at holding a pen than a hoe. Linzhan once said her hands were like silk, tender and delicate.

The only time Ahmam ever worked in the field was when she and her mother carried bamboo baskets on their back to cut the basil leaves many years ago. Ahmam remembered that day the field was enveloped by thin fog and she was in a good mood. When they still raised ducks, Jinju would send her to dig up earthworms to feed their ducks. She filled a basket with earthworms and spread them in front of the ducks, all the ducks stumbled forward and fought to eat.

Moonlight was now filtering through the trees. The early signs of spring shone through the tips of the tree branches. Ahmam took off her coat and the memory of her dad's rough shirt made from a rice bag re-emerged. When her father was in a state of delirium in the hospital, he once spoke like a prophet. "If heaven agrees without man's agreement, or man agrees without heaven's agreement, neither case works. It only works when both God and man agree." But what's heaven? The sky over their heads? Ahmam believed what her dad meant must be more sophisticated than she could guess. The first New Year without her dad and Ahmam actually felt closer to him.

Ahmam wondered if she could leave a mark on these desolate woman islands, like the plaque inscribed by Emperor. Jiaching "Writing is an outdated business!" Jinju's words sounded in her ears. The confinement over her thoughts would have never been lifted if she had never left. The south was equal to her mother. In a dreamlike state Ahmam's mom's image became one of the twelve madams Ahmam had seen in a temple parade when she was a little girl. In the choking smoke of firecrackers, all the masks of the twelve madams kept the same smiles. In the magnificent parade, Jinju, went through the crowd like an agile tiger approaching the two-meter high God of Clairvoyance and God of Clairaudience to grab the two strings of cookies they carried. When she handed the cookies to little Ahmam, she wore a triumphant expression that Ahmam will never forget. "Eat them." She commanded. The blessed cookies will make you grow taller and prettier." Jinju's eyes moved shrewdly, detecting another opportunity to grab more blessed food. The smiles of the twelve madams overlapped her mother's. It was not real, but it was what Ahmam remembered best about her mom from her childhood. Looking around the bleak village as it was bathed in moonlight, Ahmam had an image of its women. Each woman was pictured as an island wafting in the waves. Over the years, these islands had nourished and protected the lives living on them.

Ahmam's thoughts were interrupted by the traffic radio channel. It reported that northern Taiwan was in heavy rain and fog. Ahmam remembered one fortune-teller had told her that she would be very successful if she stayed in the south. She knew her drifting like a floating island in Taipei actually helped her to see through things she couldn't understand about the south before. Ahmam realized had she not experienced so much in the north, she would not have survived the burdens her family had carried.

Suddenly Ahmam felt she could finally see the light through the thick fog that had blinded her before. She shouted her name to the earth: "Chun-Mam!" A tumult response came back from the forest to her. Ahmam held her breath and listened. As the first rains prepared by the heavens for these woman islands was about to fall after a long, gloomy winter.

About the Author

Chung Wenyin was born in Yunlin, Taiwan. She holds a bachelor's degree in Mass Communication from Tamkang University. In addition to being a writer, she is a painter and a photographer.

Before devoting herself to writing literature, Chung worked as a production still photographer and script clerk. She later worked as a newspaper reporter, covering the arts and cinema. She has published essays in several prominent journals in Taiwan.

Wenyin decicided to become a full-time writer in 2000. Her talents have been recognized quickly. Her impressive proses about family, beloved islands of Taiwan and her unusual traveling experiences have made one of the most distinguished of Taiwanese writers.

Since 1994, Chung Wenyin has been awarded more than ten literary prizes, including the 2003 Yunlin County Cultural Award and the 2005 Wu San-Lien Literature Prize, which is deemed the most important literary prize in Taiwan.

Chung's works include collections of short stories; *Two People in One Day* and *The Past*. Novels she has written: *Woman's Island*, *Over the Left Bank of the River*, *Departing Love*, and *Merciful Lover* among others. Her collection of proses include *Diary for You*, *Yesterday Reemerging*, *The Everlasting Olive Tree*, *Old Appearances of Young Ladies* and *Cities for Lovers*.

Chung Wenyin extends her writing about family in the context of Taiwan's traumatic past. Her voluminous books, encompassing more than one million characters, are the most ambitious literary works about Taiwan's history to date. Ahmam's Islands is her first novel to be published in the U.S.